SELECTED PRAISE FOR **THE GODMOTHER**

'A fabulous noir' *Le Point*

'Cayre plots so cunningly she might have written the entire French TV series *Spiral*... A film of the novel has been made with Isabelle Huppert, whose own expertise is weary sophistication... It sounds like perfect casting' *The Monthly*

'It's no surprise that this novel won France's most prestigious award for crime fiction' *PW*

'An unlikely underworld figure emerges in this suspenseful and deliciously black comic crime novel – lighter but no less Shakespearean than *Breaking Bad*' *Sydney Morning Herald*

'Magnificent... the reader roots all the while for the criminal – a woman in a man's world, battling race, age and gender while cheerfully ignoring ethics' *New York Times*

'It's a joy to visit the entire world that Hannelore Cayre conjures in the 205 pages of *The Godmother*... Witty and surprising, with zero waffle, and written entirely from the centre: character first, politics second or even third, and the story shines for it.' *Spectator*

'Rigorous – superbly plotted by an author who clearly knows the territory. Vivid, smoky dialogue and an ending that ticks all the boxes... Masterly' *Le Figaro*

'*Breaking Bad* meets *Weeds*, with a French suburban twist... Patience is one of the standout characters in this year's crime fiction crop, and you'll be rooting for her all the way' *Guardian*

THE GODMOTHER

THE
GODMOTHER

HANNELORE CAYRE

translated from the French by Stephanie Smee

Published in Great Britain in 2019 by
Old Street Publishing Ltd
Notaries House, Exeter EX1 1AJ

www.oldstreetpublishing.co.uk

First published in French by Editions Métailié, Paris, 2017

ISBN 978-1-910400-96-8

10 9 8 7 6 5

A CIP catalogue record for this title is available from the British
Library.

Typeset by JaM

Printed and bound by CPI Group (UK) Ltd, Croydon, CR0 4YY

For my children

THE GODMOTHER

Money is Everything

My parents were crooks, with a visceral love of money. For them it wasn't an inert substance stashed away in a suitcase or held in some account. No. They loved it as a living, intelligent being that could create and destroy, possessing the gift of reproduction. Something mighty that forged destinies, that separated beauty from ugliness, winners from losers. Money was *Everything*; the distillation of all that could be bought in a world where everything was for sale. It was the answer to every question. It was the pre-Babel language that united mankind.

They had lost everything, it must be said, including their country. Nothing was left of my father's French Tunisia, nothing of my mother's Jewish Vienna. Nobody for him to talk to in his *patouète* dialect, nor for her in Yiddish. Not even corpses in a cemetery. Nothing. It had all been erased from the map, like Atlantis. And so they bonded in their solitude, putting down roots in the no man's land between a motorway and a forest, where they built the house in which I was raised, grandiosely named *The Estate*. A name that conferred the inviolable and sacred trappings of the Law on that bleak scrap of earth; a sort of constitutional guarantee that never again would they be booted away from anywhere. *The Estate* was their Israel.

My parents were wops, vulgar foreigners, outsiders. *Raus. Nothing but the shirt on their back.* Like all those of their sort, they hadn't had much of a choice. Either gratefully accept any job they could get, whatever the working conditions, or else engage in some serious wheeling and dealing, relying on a community of like-minded people. They didn't take long to make up their minds.

My father was the General Manager of a trucking company that traded under the name 'Mondiale', with the slogan 'Everything. Everywhere'. You don't hear the job description 'General Manager' anymore (as in *What does your dad do? He's a General Manager...*) but in the '70s, it was a thing. It went with duck à l'orange, yellow polyester roll-neck jumpers over mini-culottes, and braid-trimmed telephone covers.

He made his fortune sending his trucks to the so-called 'shit-hole' countries of the world, with names ending in –an, like Pakistan, Uzbekistan, Azerbaijan, Iran, etc. To get a job with Mondiale you had to have first done time, because according to my father, only somebody who'd been locked up for at least 15 years could cope with being stuck in a cabin for thousands of miles, and would defend his cargo with his life.

I can still see myself as if it were yesterday. I'm standing next to the Christmas tree, wearing a little navy-blue velvet dress with my patent leather Froment-Leroyer shoes, surrounded by scarred types clutching pretty little coloured parcels in their stranglers' hands. The administrative staff of Mondiale were all of similar ilk. They consisted exclusively of pied-noirs, my father's French colonial compatriots, men as dishonest as they were ugly. Only Jacqueline, his personal assistant, added a dash of glamour to the tableau. With her large, teased-up chignon, into which she would coquettishly pin a diadem, this daughter of a man condemned to death for wartime collaboration had a flashy look about her that stemmed from her Vichy childhood.

This cheerful, unsavoury team, over which my father presided with a romantic paternalism, allowed him to engage in the covert transportation of so-called extras. So, in the years leading up to the '80s, Mondiale and its royally remunerated employees got rich, first bringing over morphine base in league with my father's Corsican pied-noir mates, then branching out into weapons and ammunition. Pakistan, Iran, Afghanistan… I'm not ashamed to say, my very own dad was the Marco Polo of the thirty glorious post-war years, reopening the trade routes between Europe and the East.

Any criticism whatever of *The Estate* was seen by my parents as a symbolic attack, to the point where even amongst ourselves we never so much as alluded to the slightest negative aspect of its position: not the deafening noise of the road which meant we had to shout to make ourselves heard; not the black, sticky dust which seeped into everything; not the house-rattling vibrations, nor the extreme peril of those six lanes which made the simple act of getting home without causing a pile-up a minor miracle.

My mother would start to slow down 300 metres before the gate, reaching the driveway in first gear, hazard lights on, amidst an angry torrent of horns. My father, on the rare occasions he was there, practised a form of vehicular terrorism in his Porsche as he braked, his V8 screaming as he decelerated from two hundred to ten in a matter of metres, forcing whoever had the misfortune of following him to swerve terrifyingly. As for me, I never had any visitors, for obvious reasons. Whenever a friend asked where I lived, I lied. Nobody would have believed me anyway.

In my child's mind, we were somehow different. We were the *People of the Road*.

Five different events, taking place over 30 years, confirmed our singularity. In 1978, at number 27, a 13-year-old boy massacred his two parents and his four brothers and sisters in their sleep with a garden tool. When he was asked why, he replied that he'd needed a change. At number 47, in the '80s, there was a particularly sordid affair involving an old man who had been locked up and tortured by his own family. Ten years later, at number 12, a 'marriage agency' set up shop; in fact, it was a prostitution network of Eastern European girls. At number 18, they found a mummified couple. And just recently, at number 5, a jihadist weapons cache was uncovered. It's all in the papers. I'm not making any of it up.

How come all these people had chosen to live in that particular spot?

For some of them, my parents included, the answer was simple. Money likes the shadows and there are shadows to spare along the edge of a motorway. As for the others, it was the road itself that drove them mad.

We *People of the Road* were different. If we were at the dinner table and heard the screeching of tyres, we would stop talking, forks suspended in mid-air. Then would come the extraordinary sound of crunching metal, followed by a remarkable calm, as other drivers, with an air of funereal restraint, processed slowly past the tangled mess of chassis and flesh those people had become; people who, like themselves, had been on their way somewhere.

If it happened outside our place, around number 54, my mother would call the fire brigade and we would leave our meal unfinished *to go to the accident*, as she would say. We would bring out our folding chairs and meet the neighbours. On the weekend, it would usually happen around number 60 where the most popular nightclub in the area had set up, with its seven different dance zones. Nightclubs mean accidents. Lots of them. It's crazy how often blind drunk people would pile into a car only to die there, carrying away with them those happy families who had set off on their holidays in the middle of the night so they could wake up at the seaside.

So, the *People of the Road* witnessed up-close a considerable number of tragedies involving the young and the old, dogs, bits of brain and bits of belly... What always surprised me was that we never heard a single cry from any of the victims. Barely a muttered *oh là là*, even from those who managed to stagger up to us out of the wreckage.

During the year, my parents would go to ground like rats within their four walls, devoting themselves to tax-saving schemes of avant-garde complexity and closely monitoring the smallest external display of wealth. In this way they hoped to keep the Beast off their scent, luring it away to fatter prey.

Once we were on holiday, though, out of the French jurisdiction, we lived like multi-millionaires alongside American movie stars in Swiss or Italian hotels in Bürgenstock, Zermatt or Ascona. Our Christmases were spent at the *Winter Palace* in Luxor or the *Danieli* in Venice, and there my mother came to life.

As soon as she arrived, she would head straight for the luxury boutiques to buy clothes, jewellery and perfume, while my father did his rounds, harvesting brown paper envelopes stuffed with cash. In the evenings, he would draw up at the front of the hotel in the white convertible Thunderbird that somehow managed to accompany us on our offshore peregrinations. The same went for the Riva, which would appear as if by magic on the waters of Lake Lucerne or the Grand Canal in Venice.

I still have lots of photos from these Fitzgeraldian holidays, but there are two that convey it all.

The first is of my mother wearing a pink-flowered

dress, posing next to a palm tree that's cutting the summer sky like a green spray. She's holding up her hand to shield her already weak eyes from the sunlight.

The other is a photo of me beside Audrey Hepburn. It was taken at the Belvedere on August 1st, Swiss National Day. I'm eating a huge strawberry melba ice cream drowning in Chantilly cream and syrup, and there's a magnificent fireworks display which is reflected in Lake Lucerne. My parents are on their feet, dancing to a Shirley Bassey song. I'm tanned and wearing a blue Liberty dress with smocking which brings out the *Patience-blue* of my eyes, as my father had taken to describing their colour.

It's a perfect moment. I'm radiating well-being like a nuclear reactor.

The actress must have sensed my immense happiness because quite spontaneously she came to sit next to me and asked me what I wanted to be when I grew up.

'A fireworks collector.'

'A fireworks collector! But how are you planning to collect something like that?'

'In my mind. I'm going to travel the world and see them all.'

'Why, you're the first fireworks collector I've ever met! *Enchantée.*'

Then she called over one of her friends to take a photograph so he could immortalise this unscripted moment. She had two copies printed. One for me and one for her. I lost mine and forgot it had even existed until I happened to see hers again in an auction catalogue, with the description: *The Little Fireworks Collector, 1972.*

That photo captured the promise of my former life: a life with a future far more dazzling than all the time which has now passed since that August 1st.

After an entire holiday racing around Switzerland in search of an outfit or a handbag, my mother would spend the evening before our departure cutting off the labels from all the new clothes she had accumulated and decanting the content of her perfume bottles into shampoo bottles in case the inquisitors at customs demanded where we had found the money for all these fancy new purchases.

So why was I called Patience?

Obviously, because you were born at ten months. Your father always claimed it was the snow that had stopped him getting the car out to come and see you after the birth, but the truth is that after such a long wait, he was devastated to have a girl. And you were enormous... five kilos... a real monster... and so ugly, half your head crushed by the forceps... When you were finally dragged out of me, there was so much blood it looked like I'd stepped on a mine. It was carnage! And for what? A girl! The injustice!

I'm 53 years old. My hair is long and completely white. It went white very young, as did my father's. For a long time I dyed it because I was embarrassed, then one day I was sick of having to keep an eye on my roots and I shaved my head to let it grow out. Today it seems to be all the rage… Whatever, it goes nicely with my *Patience-blue* eyes, and clashes less and less with my wrinkles.

THE GODMOTHER

My mouth is slightly lopsided when I speak, so that the right-hand side of my face is a bit less wrinkled than the left. It's the result of a subtle hemiplegia caused by my initial crushing. It gives me a slightly working-class look, which, together with my strange hairstyle, is not uninteresting. I'm fairly solidly built, carrying five kilos extra – after putting on thirty during each of my two pregnancies when I gave free rein to my passion for large colourful cakes, fruit jellies and ice creams. At work I wear monochrome suits – grey, black or anthracite – that are unaffectedly elegant.

I take care always to be well-groomed so my white hair doesn't make me look like some old beatnik. Not that I'm obsessed by how I look; at my age I find that sort of vanity a bit sad. I just want people to say to themselves when they look at me: *Wow! That woman's in good shape!* Hairdressers, manicurists, beauticians, hyaluronic acid fillers, intense pulsed light treatments, well-cut clothes, good quality make-up, day and night creams, siestas... I've always had a Marxist view of beauty. For a long time, I couldn't afford to be fresh and beautiful; now that I can, I'm catching up. If you could see me now, on the balcony of my lovely hotel, you'd think I was the spitting image of Heidi on her mountain.

People say I'm bad-tempered, but I think this is hasty. It's true that I'm easily annoyed, because I find people slow and often uninteresting. For example, when they're banging on about something I couldn't give a crap about, my face involuntarily takes on an impatient expression which I find hard to hide, and that upsets them. So, they think I'm unfriendly. It's the reason I don't really have any friends, just acquaintances.

There is also this: I suffer from a slight neurological peculiarity. My brain conflates several of my senses, meaning I experience a different reality to other people. For me, colours and shapes are linked to taste and feelings of well-being or satiety. It's a strange sensory experience, difficult to explain. The word is *ineffable.*

Some people see colours when they hear sounds, others associate numbers with shapes. Others again have a physical sense of time passing. My thing is that I taste and feel colours. It makes no difference that I know they're just a quantum conversation between matter and light; I can't help feeling that they form part of the very body of things. Where others see a pink dress, I see pink matter, composed of little pink atoms, and when I'm looking at it, I lose myself in its infinite pinkness. This gives rise to a sensation of both well-being and warmth, but also to an uncontrollable desire to bring the dress in question to my mouth, because for me, the colour pink is also a taste. Like 'the little patch of yellow wall' in Proust's *The Prisoner,* which so absorbs the character as he looks at Vermeer's *View of Delft.* I'm convinced Proust must have caught the man who inspired his character of Bergotte in the act of licking the painting, but then left it out of his novel on the grounds that it was just too crazy and gross.

As a child I was always swallowing plastic toys and bits of paint from walls. On several occasions I narrowly escaped death, until one doctor, more imaginative than the rest, went beyond the banal diagnosis of autism to discover I had bimodal synaesthesia. This condition finally explained why, whenever I was served a plate of food with the colours all mixed up, I would spend the meal sorting the contents, my face ravaged by nervous tics.

The doctor recommended to my parents that they should let me eat what I wanted, provided I found the food on offer aesthetically pleasing and it wasn't going to poison me – pastel-coloured candy, Sicilian cassata, profiteroles filled with pink and white cream, ice cream stuffed with little pieces of rainbow-coloured candied fruit. It was he, too, who came up with the ruse of giving me paint colour charts to leaf through and rings set with big, colourful stones that I could gaze at for hours, chewing my cheek, my mind a total blank.

Which brings me to fireworks… When those sprays of incandescent chrysanthemums appear in the sky, I experience a coloured emotion so profoundly vivid that I'm simultaneously saturated with joy and replete. Like an orgasm.

Collecting fireworks… It would feel like being at the centre of a gigantic gang bang with the entire universe.

As for *Portefeux*… well, that's my husband's name. The man who protected me for a while from the cruelty of the world and who granted me a life of delights and satisfied desires. For those marvellous years we were married, he loved me as I was, with my chromatic sexuality, my passion for Rothko, my lolly-pink dresses and my complete lack of practicality rivalled only by my mother's.

We began our conjugal life in magnificent apartments, rented with the fruit of his labour. I say *rented* deliberately – as in creditor-protected – because, like my father, my husband did business of an unspecified nature that nobody knew anything about except insofar as it afforded us a significant degree of material comfort. It never occurred to people to interrogate him on the subject, such was his generosity, his breeding, the seriousness of his manner.

He, too, made his money thanks to the so-called *shithole* countries of the world, offering consulting services for the development of national lottery systems. In short, he sold his expertise in the French system, the *Pari Mutuel Urbain,* to the leaders of African nations or Central Asian countries like Azerbaijan or Uzbekistan. You can picture the scene. I personally became very familiar with that end-of-the-road ambiance, over numerous stays in improbable international hotels, both with him and with my own family. They were the only places where the air-conditioning worked and the alcohol was decent, where mercenaries rubbed shoulders with journalists, businessmen and criminals on the run, and the peaceful ennui in the bar lent itself to lazy chitchat. Not so different, for those in the know, to the cottonwool atmosphere of the common areas in psychiatric hospitals or in the spy novels of Gérard de Villiers.

We met in Muscat, in the sultanate of Oman; the same

place he died as we celebrated our seven-year wedding anniversary.

At breakfast, the morning after our first night together, without even realising what he was doing, he buttered my toast to look like my favourite painting. A rectangle of toast, half covered with strawberry jam, plain butter on a quarter of the remaining surface, and, finally, orange marmalade spread to the very edge. *White Center (Yellow, Pink and Lavender on Rose)* by Rothko.

Unbelievable, right?

When I married him, I thought I would lead a carefree life of love forever. I hadn't the slightest inkling that anything as dreadful as an aneurysm in mid-belly laugh could lie in store. But that's how he died, opposite me, at the age of 34, at the Grand Hyatt in Muscat.

When I saw him collapse head-first into his plate of salad I felt an indescribable pain. As if an apple-corer had plunged into the centre of my body and extracted my spirit in one piece. I wanted nothing more than to run away or else sink into a merciful faint, yet there I remained, stuck to my chair, fork mid-air, surrounded by people continuing quietly with their meal.

At that very moment – at precisely that moment, not a second earlier – my life truly turned to shit.

Things got off to a flying start with hours spent waiting in an incongruous police station, surrounded by suitcases and with two little girls going crazy in the heat, under the insolent stares of the Sultanate's police officers. I still have nightmares about it: clutching my passport, doing my best to soothe my two girls who are dying of thirst, smiling feebly at humiliating comments that I'm supposed not to understand. Me – the one who speaks Arabic.

Apparently it was too complicated to repatriate my husband's body. In the end a sneering functionary gave me a permit to bury him at *Petroleum Cemetery* – the only place that would accept *kafirs* – while simultaneously debiting an exorbitant amount from my credit card.

So that's how you find yourself aged 27, alone with a newborn and a two-year-old, with no income and no roof over your head. Because it took less than a month for us to be thrown out of our beautiful apartment on Rue Raynouard with its view over the Seine. Our handsome furniture was sold, and as for our leather-upholstered Mercedes, one day the hunchbacked old erotomaniac with a string of convictions who had been my husband's driver just took off with it, leaving me and my girls stranded outside the lawyer's office.

Naturally it wasn't long before I came crashing down. I already had a tendency to talk to myself and eat flowers, but one afternoon I walked out of the Céline boutique on Rue François Ier as if in a trance, dressed head to toe in new clothes and muttering to nobody in particular, *Good bye, I'll pay later!* When two poor security dudes, all in black and with ear-pieces, accosted me before I reached the door, I lashed out and bit them, drawing blood. I was taken straight to the madhouse.

I spent eight months with the lunatics, contemplating my previous life. Like a shipwreck survivor with her gaze stubbornly fixed on the empty sea, I waited for somebody to come to the rescue. People told me to get over my grief, as if it were a kind of illness I had to be cured of at any cost, but I just couldn't do it.

My two girls, too young to have the slightest memory of their fabulous father, forced me to face up to my new life. Did I have a choice? First I counted the days, then the months that had passed since my husband's death; then one day, without even noticing, I stopped counting.

I was a new woman, mature, sad, and ready for combat. An anomaly, an odd sock. I was *the widow Portefeux*!

I separated myself from what remained of my past: from my enormous Paraiba tourmaline cabochon, my pink Padparadscha sapphire, my Fancy Blue and Pink diamond *toi et moi* ring, and my fire opal. All the colours that had accompanied me from childhood. I sold everything so I could buy myself a dreary little three-room apartment in Paris-Belleville with a view onto a courtyard that gave onto another courtyard. It was a dump where night ruled the day and colours didn't exist. The building was in keeping; an old red-brick community housing block from the 1920s with cheap finishes, overrun by Chinese who shouted at each other all day long.

Then I got down to work. Ah, yes, work… Before being written out of the *happily ever after* script by some malevolent entity, I'd had no idea what it involved. And since I had nothing else to offer the world besides an intimate acquaintance with every kind of chicanery and a doctorate in Arabic, I became a court interpreter.

After this precipitous collapse in my financial circumstances, I was always going to raise my daughters in hysterical fear of a drop in social status. I paid too much for their schools, screamed at them when they got bad marks, had a hole in their jeans or had greasy hair. I'm not ashamed to admit I was a difficult mother, not at all the nurturing type.

With their stellar academic records, my two genius daughters are now working in the services sector. I've never understood quite what their work entails; they've tried to explain a hundred times, but I tune out before I get it. Let's just say we're talking about those dumb-ass jobs where you fade away in front of some computer screen making things that don't really exist and adding nothing of value to the world. Their careers are like the words in that song by Orelsan: *No one's gonna find fixed work / even with straight As and eight years' study, you're gonna have to fight / my pizza delivery guy knows how to fix a satellite!*

But I'm proud of them, and if they were ever hungry I'd cut off my arms to feed them. That said, the truth is we don't have much to say to each other. So I'll leave it there, except to declare, loud and proud, that I love them, those girls of mine. They're magnificent, honest, and they've always accepted their fate without batting an eyelid. All of which is more than can be said for me. It seems that I am the last in the family line of adventurers.

The auctioneer charged with getting rid of all my rings after I emerged from the madhouse – *Sale of the Contents of Madame P.'s Jewellery Case, a Discerning Collector*

16

– continued to send me his catalogues filled with jewels and other magnificent objects, no doubt believing that I was some high-net-worth individual.

At night, when everybody was asleep and the house was finally silent, I would sit at my desk with a glass of Guignolet Kirsch and religiously leaf through the luxury brochures. Reading each description, examining every photograph, I would play *imagine the house burns down and you rip off the insurance company.* I adore old things: they've witnessed the lives of so many people and you never get tired of looking at them, the way you do with new things.

It's remembering details like this which makes me realise that even in the depths of my grief, I've always been open to positive ideas. I've never felt desperate enough to contemplate suicide; for that you need a spiritual strength I've just never had.

To get to the point: more than twenty years after scattering all I held dear to the winds, I stumbled across the photo of *The Little Fireworks Collector,* valued between 10,000 and 15,000 euros.

Obviously I had to buy it back.

On the appointed day I turned up at Artcurial auctioneers at the end of the Champs-Elysées. I was scared to death. Scared I'd miss out on the print, that the price would soar out of my reach. Scared of all those well-dressed people having fun with their money. Scared of being outed as an impostor in my pathetic chalk-coloured suit, with my expression to match.

I hung back until it came to my lot. It was an original colour print, showing the Belvedere terrace, 50cm x 40cm. The decor was typical of the 1970s: stone, glass and blonde wood furniture. In the background, a firework was about to explode into the deep-blue sky. Audrey Hepburn was wearing a magnolia-pink Givenchy dress. Her face was right next to mine, and in the foreground, in pride of place, sat my strawberry Melba ice-cream. Everything was exactly as it should be; the absolute perfection of a moment fixed in time forever.

— Lot 240, an unpublished and unique shot by Julius Shulmann in a departure from his usual Californian villas… *The Little Fireworks Collector, 1972.* This is an original print given to the actress and not catalogued in the Paul Getty collection. Everybody will have recognised Audrey Hepburn next to that pretty little blonde girl with the blue eyes in front of her beautiful ice cream. I have 10,000 euros… 11,000, 11,500, 12,000, 13,000…

I panicked. I felt like screaming: *Stop! That little girl with the golden skin – that's me! Look at me, look what I've become! Can I not at least be allowed this?*

At 14,500, the bidding stalled… *once, twice… 15,000,* I cried… *15,000 at the back of the room…* and my rival, a guy who looked young enough to be my son, gestured that he was done.

With the fees I got it for 19,000 euros. Me, the little court translator, who prided herself on never using credit – I'd cracked for a photo.

I went home with my treasure and hung it opposite my desk. My daughters simply couldn't understand why on earth I'd suddenly bought this portrait of a cheerful little blonde girl to decorate the living room, when the rest of our apartment – apart from the pink carpet with orange flowers – had always been so grim. Had I told them I'd indebted myself for the next five years, they would have thought I'd lost my mind. Not for one second did they make the connection with their mother.

How sad is that?

I started my career as an interpreter in the summary courts.

You should have seen me in those days. I put such heart into my work. I thought I was indispensable, bending over backwards to translate each nuance and register, everything the defendants wanted to express to those who sat in judgement over them.

I felt infinitely sorry for many of the Arabs whose words I reproduced in those trials. Men who were extraordinarily poor, with little education; impoverished migrants looking for an El Dorado that didn't exist, forced into a life of small-time criminality and petty theft so as not to die of hunger.

It didn't take me long to realise that nobody was interested in my nuance or my register. The interpreter was simply a tool to accelerate the act of repression. You only have to listen to how the magistrates speak during these hearings, not varying their delivery one iota regardless of whether or not the interpreter is keeping up, regardless of whether or not the guy in the box is following.

I was an evil rendered necessary by the principles of human rights, nothing more. My presence was given barely a grudging acknowledgment – *is the interpreter here? Yes? Good, then we can start…* – before the process got underway. *You're charged with having committed in Paris and, in any event, within the relevant statutory limitation period… blah… blah… blah…* And so on, without drawing breath, for the next ten minutes.

It was particularly moving to watch my colleagues who worked in sign language, as they gestured furiously like short-circuited robots in an effort to translate a tiny fraction of whatever they had managed to grasp. Yet if one of us were impertinent enough to ask for a pause to make ourselves understood by the poor wretch for whom we were responsible (and who wasn't picking up a damned thing), the magistrate would adopt a pained look and close his eyes as if to say *I'm just going to hum a little tune in my head while I wait for this moment to pass.* Naturally the bothersome person in question would be marked down as a nit-picker and never asked back.

I very quickly stopped trying.

When I felt sorry for my guy, I sometimes managed to slip in a few things in Arabic amidst the torrent of words pouring from the judge. Things like: *Just tell these assholes what they want to hear so we can get this over with – you were in such a hurry to leave France and go back home, you only stole so you could afford a return ticket.*

For the more complicated cases involving several charges, when I had phone taps to translate, I sometimes invented things to help those defendants I thought were most deserving of pity. But I could also do the opposite and decide to sink them, especially when it was a matter of protecting their poor wives, naïve girls who were totally under their thumbs. As the prostitutes or mistresses stacked up, those bastard husbands, whose filthy intimacy I shared through my headphones, treated them like dogs. The cynicism of these men knew no bounds, as they registered their business phone lines, the cars they used for their trafficking, and the property they acquired with laundered cash in their wives' names. I made sure to tell these women what I had heard over the telephone intercepts, to show them what idiots they were being so at least they would stop showing up twice a week in the visitors' room laden with sacks of their husband's laundry, like mules.

Another thing: I was paid under the table by the government department employing me, which meant I had no taxable income.

True karma, indeed.

It's quite frightening when you think about it, that the translators and interpreters upon whom the security of the Nation rests – those very people engaged in simultaneously interpreting the plots cooked up by Islamists in their cellars and garages – are working illegally, with no social security, no pension… Frankly, you could devise a better system, couldn't you, in terms of incorruptibility.

Well, I find it pretty disturbing. And I have been corrupted.

*

At first I thought it was funny, then one day I wasn't laughing any more.

I was helping a poor Algerian in a compensation claim for wrongful detention. These cases are heard in civil courts, with lawyers arguing about the damages the State should pay an innocent person for having ruined his life. On this particular day, the parade of legal errors was being played out before an especially loathsome magistrate who eyed each claimant with a mocking sneer, as if to say *You, innocent? What else am I supposed to believe?*

The Arab in question, a labourer who had been cleaning the façade of a building where some crazy woman was living, had done two and a half years of a custodial sentence for a rape he hadn't committed, before being acquitted by the Assize Court when the lunatic retracted her accusation.

He bent my ear for a whole hour before the hearing, trying to explain how much the occasion meant to him, thinking that here, at last, was a chance to pour out everything he had held pent up inside: the promiscuity rife in the prison, the treatment reserved for sex offenders like him by his fellow inmates, the two showers a week, his wife who had returned home with his children to the *bled,* the village in Algeria, his family who didn't speak to him anymore, the flat he'd lost… He had so much to say. The court could have taken five minutes to listen to him, if only by way of apologising for the fact that some investigating magistrate had totally fucked up his life by remanding him in custody for 30 months without any evidence. But no, the Chief Justice cut him off contemptuously: *Monsieur, at the time you were working without any papers. You have no grounds upon which to make any claim whatsoever. As far as we are concerned, you don't even exist!*

I was so utterly ashamed I could no longer find the words in Arabic. I couldn't even look him in the eye. I started babbling something and then it just came out, all on its own: *Your Honour, I, too, am working without any documentation, and for the Department of Justice no less. So, since I don't exist, see how you manage without me!* And I walked out, leaving them all to it.

Despite my disillusion, I made dazzling progress on the career front. My colleagues will say I must have slept with a lot of people. Or in the cruder version that made it back to me: *there must have been kilometres of cops' dicks involved*, etc., etc.

It's true that the police decide which translator will be called to translate the telephone intercepts or interviews of those they are holding in custody. To get started as a translator, all you have to do is *swear solemnly and sincerely to assist in the exercise of justice*, which is one reason why you see all sorts in this job. You should understand that a lot of French interpreters of North African origin only know their parents' dialect, whereas there are seventeen different Arabic dialects that are as removed from each other as French is from German. It's impossible to know all of them if you haven't studied Arabic seriously at university level. So let's say we're talking about the intercepts of a Syrian or a Libyan, and they've been translated by, say, a Moroccan model, or a cop's Tunisian wife, or a police superintendent's Algerian personal trainer... How should I say this? I'm not judging, but I'd like to see them.

I think I owe my success partly to my availability, but most of all to my name. *Patience Portefeux*. Especially now that every Arab is seen as a potential terrorist, since the attacks. *Quis custodiet ipsos custodes*? Who will guard the guardians? Who will keep tabs on the Arab translators? Uh... nobody! All you can do is pray that they remain immune to the verbal abuse which they and their children are forced to suffer... A paranoid, racist society forced to trust its foreigners. It's a farce!

They were always on the phone with offers of work, and I have to say, in almost 25 years, I never turned down the smallest job, even if I was sick. Then, thanks to the respect I'd earned by my reliability, they started offering only the kind of work I wanted, leaving the rest to less experienced translators.

Little by little, I was able to steer clear of interpreting in court or in interrogations, and concentrate instead on translating phone-taps for the drug and organised crime squads. I no longer had to consort with people who only wanted to tell me all about their trials and tribulations, them in their handcuffs, and me the first and only person in the assembly line of repression to speak their language. Unlike left-wing paternalistic bourgeois types, I've never felt the need to hang out with nice Arabs in order to justify my existence. There are all sorts of Arabs, just like there are all sorts of people the world over. Polite, well-mannered types and disgusting pigs. Progressive ones and stone-age hicks from the village. Lonely, lost souls and entire villages of young people who've only been sent to France to commit crimes and bring the money back home. Like I say, all sorts.

Once I even tried my hand at terrorism, but I didn't last long – it gave me dreadful nightmares. The older I get, the less violence I can take. The beatings by the cops right under my nose, as if I didn't even exist. The spitting in the face and the insults. *You filthy whore of a traitor!* Or: *you harki bitch!* The raids where I was made to stand in the front-line outside the door without so much as a bullet-proof vest, so I could shout in Arabic: *Police! Open up!*

At some point, enough was enough.

Mainly I translated telephone intercepts: for the drug squad at 36 Quai des Orfèvres, for the Central Bureau for Illicit Drug Traffic Control in Nanterre, or for criminal investigations at the Second District of the *police judiciaire,* aka the DPJ. But with technological progress, and because I'm *Patience Portefeux*, the-French-woman-who-speaks-Arabic – that is, a woman above suspicion – I was allowed to withdraw to my own home and work on audio files at my computer. And when my mother had her stroke and my daughters wisely fled my cantankerous presence to rent with friends, I shut myself away like a hikikomori.

It was around this time that I threw myself into

translating the inane conversations of drug traffickers. To afford the 3,200 euros a month I was being charged by the nursing home where I'd had to send my mother, I was forced to churn through them at a rate of knots. Translation pays if you work like a dog. You get 42 euros for the first hour, 30 euros thereafter, and when you calculate the number of hours yourself, you quickly arrive at quite a tidy sum. You also end up with a head about to explode – with horror stories often, because it's the interpreters who filter out the baseness of human nature before the police and judges have to confront it.

I'm thinking in particular of the death agonies recorded on mobile phone that I once had to listen to during a case involving a settling of scores. Did anybody rush me off to a psychologist to look after me? And yet it was truly awful.

Asba, Patience, fissa – just do the translation, and hurry up about it...

Just one of the many reasons I couldn't give a shit about any of them.

At work I mostly hung out with cops. A lot of them are just like they are in the movies: always really angry because they can never get on top of anything, ever. Guys with deplorable domestic hygiene whose female companions have departed a long time ago and whose evenings, if they're not spent wiping their own arses, end in lousy screws with sad, lonely women. I've always kept these types at a distance by insisting on being known as *widow Patience Portefeux*, as the law entitles me to do.

True, it takes people by surprise, but it does command a certain respect.

Because I'm not some sad, lonely woman. I'm a *widow*.

I owed my working conditions to a divorced cop by the name of Philippe, who lived with his son. I met him next door to the Nanterre Drug Squad Bureau one day when I'd been called in to help. It was at a supermarket check-out, to be precise, where he was buying hot-dogs in plastic packages. I'm not at all the sort of woman who flirts, but it made me laugh, seeing those sausages stuck into their little pre-cut rolls. I couldn't resist making a comment, along the lines of *'Excuse me, but I've always wondered who could possibly buy those things?'* 'A single cop,' was his answer, smiling, and we had a laugh… Then we slept together.

He wasn't the reason my services were constantly in demand, but I did owe it to him that I was paid by the hour and was trusted to work from home.

He was only ever good to me, and I behaved very badly towards him. Though it has to be said, his unfailing honesty ended up being one hell of a pain.

2

Say, what have you seen?

Intercept No. 1387: Haribo warns Cortex that he has to call Juju because he's not answering. *Intercept No. 1488:* Cortex asks Juju to bring the stuff up. *Intercept No. 1519:* Juju has no more of the chocolate but he's got some of the green. *Intercept No. 1520:* Juju needs Cortex to bring him two lots of twelve and a salad. *Intercept No. 1637:* Haribo's ordering a thousand euros of yellow and is send-ing a boy in half an hour. *Intercept No. 1692:* Haribo is at Place Gambetta, the boy isn't there. *Intercept No. 1732:* Gnocchi asks him for ten records. Cortex tells him he'll meet him in half an hour at the Balboa hookah bar…

I translated this stuff endlessly, over and over, like a dung beetle. Like one of those sturdy little black insects that use their rear legs to make balls of shit that they then roll along the ground. Well, that's about as gripping as my daily routine was for almost twenty-five years: pushing a ball of shit, losing it, finding it again, being crushed by the load, never giving up in spite of all obstacles and diversions. That was my professional life all over… My life full stop, in fact, seeing as I spent every waking hour slogging away.

On those (very rare) occasions when I mentioned my profession at dinner parties, people were uniformly fascinated by what I overheard in those conversations. A bit like in Baudelaire's poem, *Le Voyage*:

> *Show us the treasure chest of your rich memories,*
> *Those wondrous jewels of ether and stars…*
> *Say, what have you seen?*

Nothing! I've seen nothing because… well, because there really isn't anything to see.

In the beginning I would listen to all this verbal sewage with a naturalist's interest, searching for some sort of meaning that might have a bearing on my own life, but there's nothing in it that's any different to what you'd hear at the bakery. *What would you like? Anything else with that? Will that be all?* I could write a thesis on drug traffickers, that's how much I've listened to them and how well I know them. But their small lives are just like those of any suit working in an office at *La Défense* – utterly devoid of interest.

In general, they have two phone lines: the *business* line, the number of which is always changing, and the *halal* line, which is more constant, and which is dedicated to their private life. The thing is, they speak to the same people on both lines and they often mix up their phones:

29

Guy 1: *Yeah, bro, salam alaikum, bring me 10 to the hookah bar*

Guy 2 hangs up without saying a word. Guy 1 makes two, three more attempts but Guy 2 isn't picking up. Text message from Guy 1 to Guy 2: *Eh, dude, not cool not to pick up, bro…* expletive… *uh, I'll call you on the other one.*

And so the halal line is cooked. Very quickly you work out whose it is, from the calls from Dad, Mum, brothers and sisters, who don't use the moronic nicknames they give each other when they're doing business so as not to be identifiable.

Even the most paranoid ones, the ones who only communicate on WhatsApp, Telegram or Blackberry PGP, at some point, because they need to let rip about something or other, can't help picking up their regular phone line and showing themselves to be the idiots they are.

During the week, their working day starts at around two o'clock in the afternoon and finishes at about three in the morning. It basically involves them coming and going on their scooters or in their SmartCars between their supply point, the place where the deal is going down and their office at the local kebab shop or gym.

If I had to film them going about their business, I'd set it to the soundtrack of Louis Armstrong's *What a wonderful world*.

All their conversations revolve around money: the money they're owed, the money they should have been paid, the money they dream about having. And then on the weekend they go and blow that very money in the clubs – the same clubs frequented by those *La Défense* suits, who are also their clients – except when the 1,000 euro bottle of champagne arrives at their table, they tip it upside down and empty it into the ice bucket because they don't drink alcohol. Often, when they're leaving the club, they get into a fight and then they're systematically arrested and sentenced without anybody even bothering to find out if it was them or one of the suits who started it.

Like their clients, they spend their winters in Thailand, also in Phuket, but in a different part of town, namely Patong, now rechristened *The 4,000,* after the Courneuve housing development in Seine-Saint-Denis. The locals call them the *French Arabics.*

It's holiday time over there; they don't deal because just using gets you twenty years. In summer, they hit the *bled,* the village back home, with the family. They don't deal there either, for the same reasons.

Their favourite films are *Fast and Furious 1, 2, 3,* etc, up to *8,* and *Scarface.* They're all on social media – whether they're in the slammer or on the outside – and from their posts you'd think they were working at Louis Vuitton and studying at Harvard. They exchange grand statements in which Sunni Islam (the part relating to polygamy, mainly) is cut with Tony Montana's cult comebacks and lines from rappers with over five hundred million YouTube views.

As for their capacity for introspection, they're like business people the world over. Grossly lacking.

… and I think to myself, what a wonderful world…

It may not sound like it, but I feel something approaching affection for some of them. They remind me of my father's brand of right-wing anarchism and, like him, they speak the universal language: *money*.

So, I'd been working on phone taps for the drug squad for a while, translating the shockingly bad Arabic with which the dealers punctuated their speech, thinking nobody would be able to understand them.

Generally speaking, I'm working on four to five cases at any one time. They're usually the result of a tip-off by a rival who wants to set up his own business, or a local resident fed up with the constant comings and goings of dealers outside their place.

One of these cases was generating a lot more work than the others. The protagonists, of Moroccan origin, spoke only in Arabic, which meant I had to translate the whole recording and not just a few words here and there as was usually the case.

It involved short-supply-chain dope dealing, straight from small grower to consumer, a far cry from the *Go Fast* trafficking convoys and their elaborate protocols. Dealers from outside the usual criminal milieu, and denounced not by a competitor but by a neighbour back in the *bled* because of some dark history involving a fresh water spring. Shades of Marcel Pagnol's *Jean de Florette*, you might say.

The grower, Mohamed Benabdelaziz, lived in Oued Laou, a small Moroccan village that occupies a strategic position on the coast, at the foot of the Rif mountains with its cannabis plantations, 40 kilometres from the Spanish enclave of Ceuta. On a little parcel of just six hectares, he was growing *khardala*, a high-yield variety of grass – shortish plants, weighed down with flowers, very rich in THC – which he was harvesting himself and, rarer still, from which he was then extracting the resin and pressing it, all himself. Once the drugs made it to Spain, he was paid the entire sum owing for the cannabis in Morocco via a *saraf* – banker in Arabic – who discounted the amount payable. Having paid Mohamed in advance, the *saraf* would then be responsible for recovery from the French wholesalers via debt collectors who were as discreet as they were respected. These collectors worked for a number of drug traffickers but also for retailers who had nothing to do with that world. Once the money had been recovered, it was used to buy electrical household appliances or cars that were reimported back into the country, thereby evading the ultra-strict currency exchange controls imposed by Morocco to protect its economy.

It all operated within a sealed, exclusively Moroccan environment where everybody knew each other both in France and back in the *bled*. A short sale-and-laundering process, completely modelled on the real economy. From farm to table, just like the champagne socialists' baskets of organic vegetables.

Mohamed Benabdelaziz, the producer, had his drugs transported by his nephew, a 24-year old Frenchman originally from Vitry on the outskirts of Paris.

When I first started listening to this family, the drugs were loaded onto a truck transporting vegetables. The truck crossed the border at Ceuta thanks to the complicity of a customs official cousin, then headed across Spain towards France, all the way to the *banlieue* where the wholesalers were waiting with their teams to sell it across Paris (business line).

I have to say, I'd taken a liking to all these young people. They were very different types to the immature, sociopathic trash I was used to.

Afid, in particular, the nephew of the producer from the Rif, was serious, respectful and conscientious. Another fact worth noting: he always spoke proper Arabic to his wholesalers – in this instance, his childhood mates – even though they didn't always understand everything he said (business line).

His mother was living in France. She was separated from her husband, an Algerian who had returned to the *bled* to marry a much younger woman (halal line).

Based on information I had gleaned from the thread of conversations, I had worked out that the reason Afid was speaking in Arabic, even though his native tongue was French, was to demonstrate, in his own way, that the country in which he had been raised had let him down. His dream had been to set up a workshop for luxury vehicles on the Côte d'Azur. He had done everything society had asked of him: he hadn't loitered about the place, he'd kept himself on the straight and narrow, had clearly applied himself at school where he'd received his Advanced Vocational Training certificate with distinction in auto bodywork design and manufacture. Then, on finishing his studies he had come face to face with the Great French Lie. The *educational meritocracy* – opium of the people in a country where nobody is being hired anymore, least of all an Arab – would not be providing him with the means to finance his dreams. Instead of sitting there on the steps of his housing estate block whingeing with his mates like something out of *Madame Bovary*, or providing Daesh with cannon fodder, he went off to live in his parents' homeland with his certificate in his pocket and a plan to get back out as fast as he could.

And since his uncle Mohamed was producing bricks of cannabis resin, he had found himself putting his expertise in automotive bodywork to use, making undetectable false bottoms for the trucks carrying over the family drugs (the uncle's business line, also tapped).

As for the famous garage he was dreaming of, he would open it in Dubai when he had put enough money aside.

I liked the Benabdelaziz family. They had plenty of get-up-and-go and a healthy love of life – something I myself was utterly lacking at the time, mainly due to my mother's hospitalisation. It was a period during which I did nothing but cry, sleep and work to pay for her nursing home. Putting on headphones and listening to them and their stories was one way of getting out of my miserable apartment, or the even-more-miserable offices of the drug squad. I was able to live their life vicariously, and it did me good.

I never translated their private calls, always marking them *not relevant to current investigation* – which didn't stop me following their movements just for the hell of it, as if they were daily updates from a distant branch of my own family.

Sometimes I would even go onto Google View. I would push my little arrow along the long pink road which hugged the blue sea, with one of Tinariwen's songs playing as the soundtrack. And I would imagine myself walking behind Afid to Oued Laou, sea breeze in my hair.

3

Where there's a will, the intrepid Jewish woman will find a way

When I wasn't busy following the twists and turns in the saga of my new Moroccan family's life for relaxation purposes, I would visit my mother in her end-of-the-road nursing home.

Passing through the automatic doors of that institution, poetically called *Les Eoliades*, was like crossing a border between life and an alternate universe. My nostrils were assaulted with a stench that seemed to come from the yellow walls – of vegetable soup, industrial-strength detergent and dirty mattress protectors. Parked in the hall to greet me as they waited to be nudged into the dining room, were a hundred dazed and confused old folk, waggling their heads as if saying *no* to death.

The director called them 'the residents' as though they were living in some luxury apartment building – just ordinary old people who happened to be living there, and who could leave whenever they felt like it.

Amidst this defeated humanity, I would find my mother strapped into a kind of capsule, her blind, staring eyes like saucers, fixed on the ceiling, waiting for the heavens to open like the doors of a store on the first day of the sales.

Once inside, I would take her up to her room. There, with palpable impatience, I would administer her special easy-to-swallow gruel for dysphagia sufferers. Then I would pull on her adult-sized onesie – *we don't say onesie, Madame, it's infantilising, we prefer nightwear* – purchased in ten packs on the internet. It's to stop the bedridden from rummaging in their nappies – *we don't say nappies either, Madame, we prefer protectors; nappies are for babies…* Then I would wait for the aides to move her from the capsule to her bed, as I listened to her rant.

Once she had been scooped out of that white plastic thing with a winch and deposited on her sheets, she looked so vulnerable, all curled up in her flanelette outfit, it was frankly distressing.

The woman who had once been so elegant in her lilac, chiffon dresses now had dirty teeth, a pasty mouth from her medications, a completely grey head of hair, and a face sprouting with unsightly whiskers.

I had never had a straightforward relationship with my mother. As a child I had never, for example, depicted her in my drawings with a triangle skirt, big smiling eyes and a banana-shaped smile. No, no, I always drew her as a big hairy spider with two legs bigger than the rest. Mothers with banana-smiles are what I used to call *milly-*

mummies. Milly-mummies knew how to do everything: make crepe-paper flowers, costumes for the school play, cakes with pink icing in convoluted shapes. They would come on school excursions, and would carry a mountain of coats while waiting in line without a word of complaint. Whenever anything fancy caught your eye – a crib made out of egg cartons, a treasure hunt, a chandelier made out of yoghurt containers – the response was invariably the same: *Milly's mummy did that*.

A very far cry from the ghastly yellow, shop-bought pound cake I used to bring sheepishly to every party.

No… With her gift for fiddle-faddling about, while always looking as though she was completely over-whelmed with things to do, my mother was in no way a milly-mummy. She didn't know how to cook an egg, the house was a pig sty, and as for school: *doesn't it just bore you to tears? I was lucky the Anschluss happened when it did, or my parents would have figured out that I hadn't lifted a finger for six months.*

She'd never concealed the fact that she had conceived me for the sole purpose of providing my father with a son. If he'd left her after the disappointment, I think she would have had me adopted there and then.

For all that, she was neither crazy nor completely blasé, and since she expected absolutely nothing from life, none of her hopes had ever been dashed. As a young woman, her one hope had been that she wouldn't be killed. Once a week, people from her camp were rounded up onto a train, and she would stand with her mother in a circle marked with the first letter of her last name, Z.

By the time the guards made it to O, P, sometimes as far as U, there would be no more room in the carriages, and after a few hours waiting amidst the terrified screams, the families being torn apart and the summary executions, the two women would return to their barracks. Having survived that test, she had decided that the world could get along fine without her... The world, the household, her husband, her child... all of it! Everything would just pass by her for evermore. Like a little roving satellite, she would approach life's significant events, circle around them, then head off again as quickly as possible, until in the end she no longer worried about anything at all.

Throughout her life, she didn't buy a single truly personal item; only clothes, perfume and make-up. In the mornings she would spend hours dolling herself up and examining herself soberly in the mirror; then she would plonk herself down in her flouncy dress, looking badly miscast against the medieval-style decor opted for by my father according to the principle: *if it's old, it must be tasteful...*

There she would smoke her Gallias and read novels that were an infinitely repetitive variation on the same theme: a Jewish woman leaves Austria, Poland or Russia, disembarking, bare-foot, at the base of the Statue of Liberty on Ellis Island, and thanks to her cunning nature, her ass, her good fortune, becomes a famous publisher, a renowned fashion designer, a feared lawyer... This Jewish female bulldozer crushes everything in her path, men in particular. Her children loathe her. She dies alone, but widely envied and very rich.

And my mother, sitting on a kneeler that had been

turned into a chair, illuminated by a helmet that had been turned into a lamp, would anxiously light up her Gallias in rhythm with the peregrinations of her Jewish heroine, interrupting her reading with little untranslatable exclamations.

My father – who incidentally was on first-name terms with every prostitute from around the Church of the Madeleine – would gaze proudly at her, and pronounce her like a work of art: very beautiful, but in terms of actual usefulness, absolutely worthless.

Was it for him that she spent so much time preparing herself in the morning? She liked to say so, but it was a lie because he was almost always travelling for work. No, the truth is that she didn't love anybody.

If my mother was wrapping herself in clothes of coloured silk and the lives of intrepid Jewish women, it was so she could stand every morning on the bridge of an imaginary cruise ship, headed for the paradise to where she would have liked to emigrate after the war – Miami Beach, the city of pastel colours and buildings shaped like Italian cassatas; the city where the Ashkenazys dance day and night to Paul Anka.

Since that never came to pass, she smothered her desire in the uniformity of her days, waiting patiently for the holidays as she read her novels and smoked her Gallia cigarettes.

Towards the end, before she had her stroke, she used to spend her time scrounging money off me to buy clothes at Printemps or Galeries Lafayette and returning them the next day with the good-natured complicity of the sales assistants. *Mademoiselle, I'll just leave it on,* she used to say regally, having made the purchase; then she would go down to be sprayed with perfume on the ground floor before finishing her day at the Café de la Paix eating enormous cakes with her serviette spread out over her entire body so as not to spill on herself.

When her extended death throes began with her admission into the nursing home, I cleared out the last attic room where she had lived. Apart from a few ugly, worthless pieces of furniture, and some chipped crockery, I found a whole box of lipsticks and orange nail polish, and an impressive library of stories about intrepid Jewish women.

All that emerged from what remained of her brain after the stroke were utterly incoherent criticisms directed at me. They related to the millions of euros I was stealing, her very substantial real estate holdings which I was in the process of allowing to go to rack and ruin, and her dear Schnookie, an imaginary fox-terrier, whom I was mistreating.

I had been enduring these rebukes since the day I was born, but it had grown worse over the last decade. One morning, having spent the last centime of the fat sum of money my father had left her – the girls would have been about sixteen, seventeen at the time – she called me and, in the surprised and mildly exasperated voice of a princess who doesn't think the service is up to scratch, announced:

Patience, there's no more money in the safety deposit box…
It was the tone she might have used if she'd turned on a
tap: *Patience, there's no more water.* And it was true, all
that was left in the bank were the objects she considered
precious: a sample of her favourite lipstick to remind her
of the number of the colour, her certification of Jewish status, my father's numerous forged papers, a metal coin that-
mustn't-be-lost-because-it's-very-important but which
nobody knew anything about anymore, the collars of each
of her dead dogs… but not a trace of the pile of gold coins
that her far-sighted husband had left her after his death.

There's no more money… It was as if she were describing to me a regrettable plumbing phenomenon for
which nobody in particular was to blame – especially
not her. No particular accusation, no hostility. Just:
there's no more money… Immediately, of course, she
started sponging off me, without for a moment imag-
ining that it might cause me any anxiety or that I might
have to slave away to earn this money. Worse, it was as
if she were secretly cursing me for keeping her from
penury because in becoming poor she also became
completely infuriating, constantly asking me for sums
of money down to the precise cent, along the lines *I
need 223 euros 90,* and if I ever dared provide the exact
change, she would get on her high horse and accuse me
of being a cheapskate or of treating her like a beggar.

I came away from these visits to the end-of-the-road
hotel utterly wrung out, every time.

As I waited for the lift while all the old fogies were
being taken back to their rooms, I'd sink onto a narrow

couch and wallow in the misery of the situation, of my life, of life in general, a misery that crashed down onto me as if the cable holding it up had snapped.

After every visit, consumed by self-pity at the outrageous hand fate had dealt me, I used to weep, weep with impotence, again and again... And with each outbreak of emotional incontinence, the staff would feel obliged to console me and I would feel embarrassed – even though a sentiment like shame admittedly borders on inappropriate in a nursing home.

There's a Jewish song that verges on the ridiculous it's so Jewish, which neatly illustrates my state of mind during that time:

Wejn nischt, wejn nischt
schpor dir trern chotsch dich kwelt,
wajl dos leben hot nor tsores
oj wi schlecht, wen trern felt.

Don't cry, don't cry
Spare your tears when you're in pain,
For life has only suffering
True grief is when no tears remain.

It was right there on that couch that my adventure began.

Madame Léger, an Alzheimer sufferer convinced she was on her way to her job as head seamstress at the fashion house of Balmain, was scurrying past me, back and forth. At first, I thought she had come to visit a relative, she was so dolled up to the nines. In fact, this woman who was so elegant, with her handbag over her shoulder and her high heels, was what was known as *a roaming resident*. A patient perpetually on the move, driven by the obsessive need to be going somewhere. Given the topography of the place – it was essentially a circular corridor – the poor woman went around and around like a goldfish in a bowl, her memory wiped after every circuit.

She must have taken me for one of her seamstresses who was slacking off because every time she went past, convinced she was catching me out for the first time, she made some unpleasant remark before heading off on another round. *Dear girl, do stop crying. You have two left hands, you're just not cut out for couture, that's all there is to it... Get back to work instead of behaving like a prostitute!* Another loop and there she was, back again!... *What do you think this is? Do you think you're being paid to take endless cigarette breaks... Get back to your work...* Generally, by the third round, I would have stopped crying, and by the fifth, I was having a good laugh, which then elicited threats of being sacked for insubordination from my demented chief seamstress.

I got along well with her two children who were slogging away, like me, to pay for the costs of that wretched establishment. Poor things, they had not one, but two institutionalised parents. A mother with Alzheimer's and a bedridden father. The cost of the whole exercise? More than 6,500 euros a month for this 20th-arrondissement institution that really had nothing luxurious about it whatsoever.

The carers, once they had settled everybody else on the floor, would then set about capturing the wanderer so they could undress her and force her into bed. Strapped in, she would cry out, calling for help, railing against her confinement... It was at that particularly ghastly moment that I would choose to clear out.

But one day in April, Madame Léger escaped.

I was the first to notice. Having been left to laze around on my couch with complete impunity, I asked one of the cleaning ladies, between sobs, if something had happened to her.

You're right, yes, where has she got to, that Madame Léger? came the response from the kindly African woman in her *Côte d'Ivoire* accent you could cut with a knife. She immediately sounded the alert and all the staff set off to look for her. Every room and all the common areas were methodically searched, in vain. No more Madame Léger. She had made a dash for it, ripping off her wander-control device like the raptor in *Jurassic Park*.

The brain of an Alzheimer sufferer can be likened to an onion that will rot layer by layer, from the outside in. *The desire for freedom is hidden deep in the centre, at the core*, I said to myself as I made my way through the hub-bub provoked by her disappearance.

The next day, while listening to the conversation between Afid's mother and her son on the halal line, I heard the exact same story coming straight from her mouth.

I already knew she was a carer in a nursing home in Paris, but not in a million years had I imagined that fate could have landed her at *Les Eoliades*, at the bedside of my very own mother.

It took me a good week to identify her, given that in all these old people's homes, like in the hospitals and child-care centres, practically the only people working there are blacks and Arabs. *Racists everywhere, know this – the first and last person who will spoon-feed you and wash your intimate parts is a woman you despise!*

I identified her by the fact that at 6.55pm, whatever else was going on, she would shut herself up in the plant room to take her son's call – a call whose timed and date-stamped file I would receive the following day.

She had to be up to speed with his business affairs. And yet, to listen to their candid chats through my head-phones in the evenings, you could truly wonder if any-body in that family knew that drug trafficking was an illegal activity in France, attracting severe penalties.

Up to then I hadn't paid much attention to her, but I rec-ognised the woman as one of the nurses who would from time to time offer me a tray of Middle-Eastern sweets as I wept on my couch. Since she worked the day shift and I came mostly in the evenings, I had never spoken to her properly – just the usual hello and goodbye. It must be said that when you find yourself in that sort of place, face to face with your own mortality, you don't really feel like making conversation. Anyway, what is there to talk about? Apart from wee and poo and death… Unless you're completely deranged, you enter a nursing home with the single thought of getting out again as quickly as possible.

She was a little older than me, Moroccan background,

always smiling, and she wore a headscarf – which, by the way, is perfectly acceptable and tolerated when the activities of the Muslim in question are confined to cleaning and wiping up after the elderly.

Out of curiosity I brought my visiting hours forward a little, and began to observe her more closely.

Khadija – that was her name – came to speak to me of her own accord as I was trying to make my mother swallow some substance the colour of jellyfish. I'd hardly been there five minutes and I already felt like squashing the container into her face.

Gently, she took the spoon out of my hands.

'If your Mum doesn't want to eat, it's because she can feel you're all tense. You're going to break your teeth, you're clenching them so tightly when you bring the spoon towards her. Old people are like animals, they pick up on everything.'

Just then my mother seemed to confirm this analysis by looking me up and down like a hostile, old tortoise from deep within her capsule-carapace.

'Look at her, she's refusing to open her mouth out of sheer stubbornness!'

'Stroke her as you offer her something to eat… you'll see, she'll relax.'

And she did exactly that, stroking her hand over my mother's sun-spotted, shrivelled arm.

'I can't do that!' I said, petrified with disgust.

'It's okay – that's what we're here for!'

'Nobody should have to live like this… Not her and not me. It's horrible to end up like this!'

'But you know, when you're not here, your Mum's not as annoying as all that. In fact, she's quite cheerful. What do you say, my princess?'

And she kissed my mother who had already completely forgotten I was there and was crooning in Yiddish, her face half-paralysed:

'*Ikh bin a printsesin!*'

'She tells us lots of stories. She talks about wonderful parties when your father was Ambassador in Miami. The guests, the champagne, the beautiful dresses, the palm trees… all of it… it lets us dream a little… takes us out of ourselves.'

The suffocating irony of the situation made me feel a bit better.

I smiled. 'We're not very good at affection in our family.'

'But I know from what she tells me about your life, about your daughters, all of that, that she has always been there, with you.'

'Yes, there's no denying that. She has always been very much there… in her own way, let's just say.'

'You're both angry about what's happening and that's normal. Your mother, she can tell she's slipping away, so she's grabbing on to anything she can, including you, and it makes her unbearable. She's scared of her life ending and you're scared too. It's a difficult time, always tricky. And it's why we're here, so it's easier for the families and, if you won't mind me saying, there's no point you coming here every day. At some point you won't be able to stand it anymore, and afterwards, you'll only have bad memories of her. We're looking after your mother very well, and if there's a problem, we'll call you. Go on, go home.'

That evening, I didn't weep on my couch. I even invited my two girls over for dinner and made them what my mother used to call her culinary speciality: *Girls, with this recipe, you'll be alright, whatever the circumstances.*

> *Miami salad*
> *One tin of palm hearts, one tin of corn and one tin of sliced pineapple.*
> *One avocado*
> *Dice the ingredients.*
> *Put everything into a salad bowl.*
> *Add some peeled defrosted shrimps.*
> *For the cocktail sauce: stir together some Heinz ketchup and Amora mayonnaise until it's salmon-pink.*

It would be an exaggeration to say that we became friends that day, Khadija and I, but she was so kind, so patient with the old people and their families, that she allowed me to get past my internal guilt about not doing anything useful. I followed her advice and spaced out my visits.

Towards the end of June, things got more complicated.

For a couple of months I had been fairly vague in my translations about the quantities being imported by her son, Afid.

In the first wire taps, he had been bringing in 50 kilos per trip in his little vegetable truck, like an unassuming ant; then it was 60, then 70... At some point, I stopped translating, allowing the specifics to go unremarked, and making the note *indecipherable* in my reports on the very rare occasions when the quantity was mentioned. In April, they were talking 250 kilos, and by May they had acquired a bigger truck.

I was only given the conversations with some Arabic to translate, but I knew that the drug squad detectives were listening to the wholesalers who were chatting amongst themselves and with their customers in French. Afid's mates were all very suspicious and limited themselves to announcing *fresh delivery* by SMS, and nothing more. I guess they couldn't be sure of the exact quantities before they took delivery.

The Benabdelaziz family had invested in a second-hand Crompton at the end of April, a semi-inflatable, flat-bottomed motor boat that would take them across the Spanish border by sea, with the new truck being permanently parked at Ceuta.

I made sure to mention this detail of the new boat in my transcripts, since the whole world, both in Morocco and France, was talking of nothing but the purchase and the *mad rides* – their words – they'd all be able to go on, out on the water in summer, even if Afid did dampen their enthusiasm each time by pointing out that the vessel was intended for work purposes.

Afid was planning a crossing in July, and this time he wouldn't be alone, but accompanied by one of his uncle's employees. A team of *aquadores*, specialising in the unloading of drugs, would be waiting for him on the beach at Calamocarro at Ceuta, their job being to secure the landing location and move the drugs as efficiently as possible to the false-bottomed truck.

Given all these reinforcements, the drug squad was anticipating a significantly larger quantity than normal.

Out of curiosity, I had watched a YouTube clip about how these disembarkations were managed. You could see this new breed of beach 'attendants' shifting the cargo in broad daylight and with complete impunity smack in the middle of swimmers who were filming it all on their mobile phones.

Once the drugs were in the truck, the two men were planning to take it to a warehouse located near Vitry, not in a *Go Fast* convoy with other vehicles, but on their own, discreetly, driving at a grandfatherly pace in their vegetable lorry. Waiting at Vitry would be their three usual mates, plus two other wholesalers with their vehicle. On the return journey, Afid intended to use the truck to pick up his mother and sister and take them back to the *bled* for the summer holidays.

Sensing a big catch, the police had decided to arrest them in the act – just, as they put it, so they could *stamp on those piss ants* before heading off themselves for a holiday in the sun.

At this point the utter absurdity of my situation sank in. Here I was blithely falsifying telephone intercepts – whether out of sheer bloody-mindedness or a desire to please the mother of the drug trafficker who had not, in fact, asked me to do any such thing – while in some parking lot at Vitry they were going to uncover I don't know how much superior quality, so-called *olive* hash selling for up to 5,000 euros a kilo.

The departure from Spain was fixed for the evening of 13th July so they could get to France on the 14th, the national holiday, and head up to Paris with non-existent surveillance given the massive mobilisation of security forces that happened every year on that day under France's Vigipirate anti-terror alert system.

At this stage of the investigation, there was no more translating at my place. I was summoned into police headquarters at Quai des Orfèvres on the 13th at around 10pm and told to stay until the truck got to Poitiers in the afternoon of the 14th. Then, at around 4pm, with everything on track, I was allowed to go home, take a shower, and sleep a few hours so I would be ready to translate the questioning of the Moroccan driver.

In a state of panic, I ran to the nursing home.
I found Khadija and dragged her into the plant room, where I briefly told her, in Arabic, who I really was, what I had done and what I knew. I urged her to call her son, who should have made it to Orleans or thereabouts by then, bearing in mind when I had left the squad's offices.

She looked at me, aghast, but didn't say a single word to interrupt me. When I had finished, she did what I said and set out the situation for him in splendid summary and with a magnificent sense of composure.

'Be quiet and listen: there's a lady standing in front of me who speaks Arabic and who's saying you have to get off the motorway and hide the little fish somewhere. After that you have to get back on the motorway and you can't warn the others, because otherwise they're going to dig around and they'll know it's me and the lady who warned you. They're waiting for you at Vitry. Please, don't resist.'

Meanwhile I had the A-10 up on my mobile.

'Ask him which is the next motorway exit.'

'The lady's asking which exit you're at exactly.'

'I've got the 14 – Orleans North coming up.'

'Tell him to throw his phone out the window immediately and only get off at exit 12, otherwise they'll pinpoint him by the coordinates. The Saint-Arnoult toll booth is at exit 11 and the police have stationed two surveillance vehicles there.'

'You've got to throw your phone out right now and then take exit 12 to hide the fish, you hear me? Exit 12! After that you won't be able to get off.'

'Bye, Mum,' he said to his mother, hanging up.

Khadija stared at me, eyes wide with fear, then burst into tears.

I had a lump in my throat.

I held her tightly in my arms and we sat down to wait, huddled up against each other, holding our breath, eyes and ears directed towards the door, our minds even further away, alongside the police who were waiting for Afid.

At some point, I finally stood up and went to visit my mother.

*

Afid obeyed and was arrested as expected when he reached the five wholesalers who were still waiting for him patiently at Vitry, despite the fact he was grossly late. Needless to say, the officers found only an empty hiding place – no doubt rapidly discovered by Platoon and Laser, the two Belgian Shepherds from the dog squad, who must have barked like the possessed.

At around 7 o'clock in the evening, I was summoned to translate the interview of the courier from the village, who only spoke Moroccan dialect. I went in, my spirit light, with no sense of culpability or dread, but rather, I'd say, with a kind of cheerful detachment.

When I arrived at the drug squad offices, I found the usual hive of activity. Detectives who hadn't slept for 48 hours were frenetically going from one room to another with statements from the most forthcoming interviewees, which were then used to trick the most reticent. Apart from Afid, the courier and the five wholesalers who were waiting for the merchandise, the police had arrested a dozen collaterals – girl-friends, parents and a few dealers, each of whom was being cooked in a separate room. Khadija hadn't yet been questioned, but it would only be a matter of hours because she would soon finish her shift and they were waiting for her outside her apartment block.

Young men, all of Arabic background, were coming in and going out in handcuffs. I didn't know which one was the famous Afid until a detective pointed me out, shouting *the interpreter's here!* at the top of his voice, and a boy waiting his turn for a medical check turned to stare at me. I flushed red as a beetroot.

I translated the courier's interrogation. From his pithy responses to the questions put to him by the detective: *I don't know what drugs you're talking about… if you say so…* etc., I quickly realised that none of the interviewees would be giving up any information to speak of.

Since they had not actually found any drugs, the cops had been pretty vague about the quantity involved, though they were estimating it to be in the order of half a tonne. They weren't at all happy that all this had disappeared into thin air, even if the phone taps, baffling as they were, were enough for them to send everybody to prison.

To the question *Why did you get off the motorway so quickly and what did you do between Orleans and the Saint-Arnoult toll booth for more than two hours?* the Moroccan had replied that he was driving the truck up with Afid so they could sell it. They were supposed to be paid on delivery, but they were worried because the engine was making a strange noise. They'd spent a good two hours fixing it before returning to the motorway, where they had floored it so they wouldn't arrive late to the place where they were meeting the purchaser. *And the stash? What stash? Was there a stash? Oh, I didn't know!*

I could see the two detectives felt like hitting him, but what they might, not so long ago, have allowed themselves to do, they no longer did in the presence of my respectable fifty-year-old self. So they just stood there, harbouring death in their soul.

*

And if I had been asked to translate the call between Khadija and her son before he reached the Saint-Arnoult toll booth, I would have written what I always wrote – *Conversation not relevant to current investigation* – and naturally they would have believed me. But nobody asked me anything.

I remember going back to my place feeling completely washed out.

I undressed and stood in front of my bathroom mirror to take out my contacts. When I looked at myself I was shocked by the stony face staring back at me.

Khadija had been right when she said I was angry. It would have been no exaggeration to say that anger was flooding out of my body, like water from a sewer after a storm. I considered myself closely. My breasts, my thighs, my arms... all a lost cause. My whole body was crying out for help. I had to face facts – I was getting old.

What was to become of me, the woman with no pension, no social security? I had nothing but my waning strength. Not a cent put aside, my meagre savings swallowed up by my mother's drawn-out death at *Les Eoliades*. I pictured myself rotting, once I was no longer able to work, with nobody to care for me, in my apartment block populated by Chinese, kept awake by their unbearable shouting. Ever since their arrival, the members of the tentacular Fò family had simply looked right through me as if through a window pane, but as soon as they realised I was no longer paying my building and administrative fees, I would instantly lose my cloak of invisibility and be sent off to croak on a street corner like a pigeon.

That's what I told myself as I looked in the mirror that evening.

This ultra-realist vision of my future filled me with such despair that I was moved to apply some make up, spray myself with perfume and slip into my pretty apricot-compote-coloured dress. Not for anybody in particular. Just for me. And as I was trying to make myself feel better in front of my mirror, I heard explosions. It was only at the third explosion that I realised it wasn't an attack, but the 14th of July fireworks, which I had completely forgotten.

I hauled myself up the stairs, two at a time, to the top floor of my building. A young Chinese couple had already opened the fire escape and were cuddling up together to watch the fireworks. I went to the far side of the roof top to enjoy my trip all on my own. The *widow Portefeux*. The odd sock.

I lay down on my back, my arms spread-eagled, and there beneath the sprays of colour, waves of pleasure washed over me as I offered my body up to the heavens.

Back in my flat, I went to bed but I couldn't get to sleep, tossing and turning feverishly under my sheets, my head full of all that had just happened.

For almost twenty-five years, I had been clinging to a piece of driftwood in the tempest of this lousy existence of mine, all the while waiting for some unexpected plot development worthy of a television series. A war, a win in the lottery, the ten plagues of Egypt, whatever... And now, at last, it was happening!

As I looked at the portrait of me next to Audrey Hepburn, I told myself that my plan of collecting fireworks had shown some damned ambition... Fireworks were set off only against summer skies, so following them around the world would mean living an *endless summer* – like some cosmic surfer carried by an enormous global wave. Sydney at New Year's, then Hong Kong, Dubai, Taipei, Rio, Cannes, Geneva – and to finish, the biggest, most dazzling display in the world: Manila. Fireworks launching from one hundred different points at once, the city transformed into some extra-terrestrial battlefield.

A life plan as gratifying as that vision of the little girl with the *Patience-blue* eyes in front of her huge ice cream.

Somewhere in the vicinity of exit 12 on the A10, out in the country, there was an enormous quantity of hash that was just asking to be recovered.

I had not had much of an internal struggle before sticking my nose into the Benabdelaziz family's affairs. No struggle at all, truth be told. I'd even go so far as to say I had acted on instinct, or perhaps from some kind of deep-rooted, ancestral drive.

As for any sense of guilt, there was none – absolutely none!

Almost from day one of my professional life, I had understood that there was no logical point to my work.

Fourteen million cannabis users in France and

eight hundred thousand growers living off that crop in Morocco. The two countries are friendly, and yet those kids whose haggling I listened to all day long were serving heavy prison sentences for having sold their hash to the kids of the cops who were prosecuting them and of the judges who were sentencing them, not to mention to all the lawyers who were defending them. It didn't take long for them to become bitter and poisoned with hate. I can only think, though – even if my cop boyfriend insists I'm wrong – that this excess of resources, this furious determination to drain the sea of hash inundating France, teaspoon by teaspoon, is above all else a tool for monitoring *the population,* insofar as it allows identity checks to be carried out on Arabs and blacks ten times a day.

Regardless, drug trafficking had provided me with a living for almost twenty-five years just as it had the thousands of civil servants charged with its eradication, along with the numerous families who, without that money, would be relying on social security to feed themselves.

Even in the United States, when it came to decriminalisation, they were less idiotic than we were, and that's saying something. Over there, they were emptying the prisons to make room for real criminals.

Zero tolerance, zero thought – that about sums up the drug policy in this country, which is supposed to be governed by people who came top of their class. But fortunately, we have our *terroir*, the sacred, wine-producing soil of France. At least we're allowed to be plastered from morning to night. Too bad for the Muslims, but then all they have to do is hit the booze like everybody else if they too want to work on their inner beauty.

And I was meant to be feeling guilty? What a joke!

The woman who had been scarred on life's battlefield was finally hauling herself out of her mental inertia. *I'm done with hoping; now I want!* as Randal declared, the hero from my dad's favourite book, *The Thief of Paris* by Georges Darien. We'd always worked with Arabs in my family, so it might as well continue. It all seemed so stunningly obvious.

So, in my newly-awoken state, I returned to the daily grind of *work–nursing home–work…* A few translations in a procuring case: some girls who'd been brought over from the *bled* by some guys promising them they'd be footballers' whores. The inevitable shoulder-surfing credit card scammers memorising people's PIN and then knocking off their card: this gang were all from Boufarik in Algeria and had provided me – and themselves – with ten years of guaranteed income. A dope-dealing charge involving three charmless and spectacularly brainless Moroccans who swore *onthequranofmecca* every second breath. And finally, Khadija, whose phone had once again been tapped by the investigating magistrate.

Then, three days later, on 18 July, my mother had her second stroke.

The carers noticed that her brain had shrunk overnight to the size of a peach stone. She could no longer swallow at all, nor speak a word of French, and she just kept on screaming, terrified. Management had sent her for a scan which had confirmed their diagnosis: whatever remained of her right cerebral hemisphere was totally shot and the left side was swimming in blood.

When I went to *Les Eoliades* to ascertain the extent of the disaster, Khadija had returned to work and was sitting waiting for me on my mother's bed.

'I wanted to thank you,' she said.

Her scarf contrasted sharply with the pallor of her face, ravaged by a week without sleep, giving her an air of profound tragedy.

I reassured her in Arabic: 'It was inconceivable that I do nothing when I've been listening to you speak with your son every day. Do you have any news?'

'Yes, his lawyer has told me he's doing well and has asked me for lots of money.'

At this point she hesitated, then asked me in Arabic: 'So, you know everything about us, then?'

'I don't know about everything. I've been following your family for five months; you, your son, your brother as well as the driver who works on the farm,' I answered in French.

'That's very embarrassing.'

'It's really nothing to be embarrassed about… You've seen all my dirty laundry, too… Just look at me, unable to touch my mother, unable to change her nappy – even to make her eat a bit of yoghurt… I'm the one who should be feeling embarrassed about making such a spectacle of myself. You've done so much for her… and for me.'

Khadija started sobbing in French: 'The police, they trashed everything at my place, and talked to me like I was dirt. We're good people, Madame, we're not low-life.'

'I know, you just want your life to be a little easier. We're all in the same boat, you know.'

'My son said my brother's neighbour is the one who informed on us because we found a source of water and he hasn't. Before, we used to grow almonds on my family's land, and then my brother, when he found that cursed spring, he said to himself that he could finally grow *khardala* like everybody else because it's a crop that needs a lot of water.'

'… from which he extracts the resin and then presses it, I know all about it.'

'Yes, he's making the *tbislas* himself. It's a lot of work. At first, I wasn't at all happy because I said to myself it would only bring trouble, and then my son convinced me that with our cousin who's a customs officer, there wouldn't be any problem getting it through. You know, my son, he's very intelligent. He's always been first in everything. He has good qualifications, but nobody here wants to give him any work.'

'How long has he been doing this?'

'This is about the third crop. My brother used to tap the stalks and flowers through sieves and that would take a lot more time. It was my son who told him how to do it much faster by freezing the seedlings. You could say that it's really his, this product, he's even designed the logo himself. He's already done a lot of trips, but he had never brought in as much as he did this time… I knew it was going to end badly but nobody listens to me. Luckily my brother was able to pay back the *saraf* for our share, otherwise…'

She held her hands up to the ceiling as if to show that the family had only narrowly avoided being struck down by divine forces.

'Your share? I don't follow… '

'In the truck there was also merchandise that he was carrying for other people… And I'm certain they're following me, those people. Whenever I go anywhere I feel like I've got eyes on my back.'

'It might be the police. They want the drugs too.'

'No, no, I know what I'm talking about. Those people, they're from the *bled*. The police have told me to check into the station twice a week, like a criminal. They're not letting me see my son in prison and I'm no longer allowed to have any contact with my brother, but I don't care about that because my daughter has shown me how to talk to him using the PlayStation so nobody can listen in on us.'

We were interrupted by my mother who started to scream in bewilderment and terror, pointing her one good finger at some imaginary spot in the direction of the toilets:

'*Neyn, ikh vet nit! Neyn, ikh vet nit!*'

'Stop, mama!'

Khadija was stroking her face to calm her down.

'Poor thing, she's been like this ever since they brought her back from the hospital. Especially at night. Nobody understands the language she's speaking. She really does look like she's very, very scared.'

'It means, *I don't want to!* in Yiddish. She saw some terrible things when she was young. Please, can you give her something to calm her down… Some sort of medication that will make her sleep all day so she doesn't have to wake up anymore except to eat.'

'I don't have anything to give her unless the doctor prescribes something, but you could always bring her something and I'll take care of it. It's the least I can do.'

'The most important thing is, you mustn't change your number, otherwise they'll be suspicious and think you have something to hide. If they've let you keep your telephone, it's because they're tapping it. If they haven't found the drugs that Afid has hidden, it's because they're looking for it in the wrong place; the last place they were able to ping his phone before he ditched his mobile. Make sure you only speak Arabic on the telephone, that way they'll always have to run your conversations through me to translate them. Speak Arabic to everybody, always!'

She agreed with an air of collusion.

'Khadija, I can sell your product. True, I'm not exactly sure how, but I feel it must be possible because of my job. I've shown you that you can trust me… I need money! Everything I've earned my whole life has gone to raising my children and paying for this hospital. If I don't do something very fast, I'm going die on the streets, homeless…'

She gently placed her hand on my arm. 'Are you sure I can talk on my telephone?'

'Absolutely, that's safe.'

'Alright, I'll organise a meeting with my brother. Tomorrow.'

At the time, I didn't understand what that was supposed to mean.

When I returned to the hospital at the same time the next day with some Diazepam, Khadija called me over with a conspiratorial look and led me into my mother's room, locking the door. Then, while I was drugging her with a concoction tinted blue from twenty drops of the stuff – although the maximum dose is meant to be five – the carer plugged a game console into one of the home's laptops and started a private session on Grand Theft Auto 5.

She'd chosen a sporty young woman for my avatar, with long white hair and blue eyes, and I appeared on a military airport runway in the middle of the jungle.

A big twin-propeller aeroplane landed, and out of it emerged an older-looking man.

'Look, that's my brother,' Khadija said proudly.

Then the figure started sprinting towards me. I was totally flabbergasted. Once he had come to a stop, the two characters stood there, moving awkwardly from one foot to the other, arms dangling, in a state of suspended animation.

'Say something. He can hear you.'

'Hello. Are you… Mohamed?'

'Yes.'

The conversation continued in Arabic.

'My sister told me you wanted to speak to me.'

'I know you have no more contacts to sell your product, but I can supply you with some because of the work I do. For example, I'm currently listening in on these Moroccan guys who have a decent clientele in the south of Paris: around Nation, Vincennes, Saint-Maur…'

There was a long pause.

'I don't… I don't know them, these guys you're talking about.'

The man was a lout; barely civil.

'I'll give you their names and you can make some enquiries so you can satisfy yourself that the families are trustworthy.'

'Yeah… trustworthy…'

'If you work with these boys, there's some fat cash to be made, and fast, because I'll always be one step ahead of the police.'

Some fat cash to be made… Having regularly encountered this obscene and gluttonous term in my intercepts, I knew it had a magical effect on dealers, like attracting children with the promise of cake.

'What would you know about it? Nothing.'

'The poorest quality is worth 250-300 a kilo in Morocco and is traded for 800 in Spain once it's across the border. The Pakistani variety is being bought for 1,200 and sold for 2,500 in Spain. The olive variety – your resin – gets 1,400 in Morocco and 4,000 in Spain, because it's rare. After that, between Spain and France, it goes up on average 1,000 a kilo. As for the pollen, the *Abdallah*, you're not making it but you should, because those guys I'm telling you about have some customers with a lot of money. But I think we could ask for up to 5,000 a kilo for your drug, retail, seeing as the quality on the market at the moment is so bad.'

'Yeah…? You think?'

'And I'd take 20% of the retail price.'

'Oh, right…'

'What I'm offering you is to set up a secure, on-going organisation, with continuous supply to a whole lot of people who I'll be choosing after having tested them at length by listening in on them without them knowing. And I'm just saying – the drugs are sitting out in the open somewhere. If your nephew tells you where he's hidden them, Khadija and I can go and put them somewhere safe. You can trust me.'

'How am I supposed to know where they are? Along the road somewhere! Afid didn't send me the GPS coordinates because you had the bright idea of telling him to ditch his phone before finding a place to hide the shit. Now, because of you, I have to wait for him to make contact with me.'

'If I hadn't been there, everything would have been lost so you could say that it's thanks to me you still have your product. By the way, I don't think I've heard a thank you.'

Frankly, he was beginning to irritate me.

'Yeah…'

'How much was there?'

'To be honest, I don't even know why I'm talking to you.'

And the figure disappeared from the screen, leaving me alone in the jungle.

'My big brother is a bit old-fashioned,' said Khadija, by way of excuse.

'Meaning?'

'I think it's because you're an educated woman. He feels humiliated.'

'But that's ridiculous!'

'It's just how it is.'

'My whole life, I've copped it for being a woman.'

'Me too. But who cares… it's their problem! I like my life the way it is.'

My mother had started to smile as though she was following the conversation, despite being completely out of it. We sat there, watching her in silence.

'She told me a story… I've always wondered if it's true. At the end of the war, she caught some nasty bug and had a fever of 41 and a half. Everybody around her agreed she wouldn't make it through the night, and while they were all there, talking about how sick she was, something appeared on her pillow that looked like rays coming out of her head. They all knelt down to pray, saying she was a saint, except my grandmother who didn't believe in anything, and certainly not that her daughter had been touched by some sort of grace. She leaned in closer to get a better look at the supposed rays: they were colonies of lice leaving her head in single file because she was dying. Have you ever heard or seen anything like that?'

'No, no I never heard of such a thing.'

'Yeah, me neither.'

Two days went by, and while I was at the Second District

offices of the DPJ in the 10th arrondissement translating the interview of somebody being held in custody, my telephone started ringing insistently. The number on the display was my mother's nursing home.

In the end, in the middle of the job, I took the call, apologising profusely. It was the director.

'You have to come right away. Your mother hasn't stopped screaming the whole night. Not only that, she hit a carer, who then of course decided to take advantage of the situation and take sick leave. I think the time has come for everybody's sake for her to be admitted to palliative care. Otherwise you'll have to start paying for an extra carer.'

'Look, I can't leave work just now. I'll get a break in two hours.'

'Don't take this the wrong way, but I can't afford to have such a difficult patient. I'm managing with three carers here in circumstances where I really need double that number. We have a community here, and your mother screaming day and night upsets the other residents, especially those with Alzheimer's who are already difficult enough to handle at the height of summer.'

'But I saw her the day before yesterday... she was calm. Khadija is really good with her and...'

'Khadija has passed away!'

'What?'

'Apparently she had a heart attack yesterday evening outside her place while somebody was stealing her bag. Yes, I know, it's dreadful, we're all completely in shock. That's why, you'll understand, I have to work out a more appropriate solution for your mother as a matter of urgency. I've found her a place in geriatric palliative care. All I need is your signature.'

I finished translating the interview, concentrating as best I could, then left in a taxi for *Les Eoliades*.

When I got to my mother's floor, I found Khadija's colleagues in a complete state. The official story was that she had had a heart attack after a group of thugs apparently followed her into the building where she lived in order to steal her bag. But I had my own ideas. It had to be the other owners of the drugs her son was carrying who were responsible for her death; the men from the *bled* who she knew had been following her. Or could it be a simple case of Radio Prison having broadcast to all the dealers in the Île de France that a certain Benabdelaziz and his Vitry gang had been brought in without their fat stash of superior quality product? Whatever, some guys had gone to put some serious pressure on poor Khadija to encourage her to tell them where Afid had hidden the drugs, and her heart had given out.

So that was it. Now I was up to my ears in it, in the business. The place out the back that my father used to keep hidden from us, where the rubbish bins were kept. Those times when he would come back from one of his trips with his jaw clenched, and all of us in the house knew it'd be a good idea to just shut up…

Raging, deprived of the extra medication which Khadija had been administering to her on the sly, my mother was screaming louder than ever as she thrashed about in her bed as if she were about to drown. The sight of her dirty, uncombed hair, of her half-paralysed face, contorted by demented grimaces, was more than I could bear.

Seeing her like that, I went into *standby* mode. The only thought that popped into my mind, as I fixed the pepper-and-salt tufts of hair poking wildly out from the top of her head, was that I had never noticed a single grey hair before she had gone into hospital. I didn't even know she was a natural brunette, since I had only ever seen photos of her as a young woman in black and white.

I signed the papers presented to me by the director, whereupon, much as one might rid oneself of some large stinking animal, she called an ambulance to carry my mother off as quickly as possible to the very last square on the snakes-and-ladders board game of human degeneration: the palliative care centre.

No longer required by any commercial niceties to soften her tone, it was in a sharp, abrupt voice that she asked me to empty the room of all my mother's things so it could be cleaned and re-occupied the next day by another resident. Most importantly, I was to be quick about it. Nail clippers, hair brush, moisturiser, cushion, scarf, onesie… that was all that remained of my mother's material life. I tossed it all higgledy-piggledy into a box with the nagging feeling that I had already acted out this hideous scene several times in my life.

When I left her room, the cleaning women were already there.

All that I kept in the wake of her being spirited away

was a soft toy – a life-sized white, brown and black fox-terrier that had cost me a bomb and that had served as a substitute in her blind-woman's hands for Schnookie, her childhood dog. The rest I left behind. Then I went back to the Second District police station to finish my work.

Schnookie was the dog who had drowned in '38 when she and her family were crossing the Danube in a dinghy to escape the Germans. The fox-terrier had panicked and leaped overboard, to be swept away by the current before the eyes of my powerless mother. *It's the only time in my life I cried,* she would add, in a quavering voice to whomever was listening at the time. Needless to say, I would feel like killing her whenever she put on this display.

I took the bus with my stuffed fox-terrier toy standing on the seat next to me. I wasn't feeling very well. It must have been quite a sight, this woman with her white hair in disarray and her soft toy – two people took surreptitious photos of me to post on social media. I'd rather not think about the caption they chose to go with it.

Once I got back to work, I went and sat down in the break room that was plastered with posters of bad cop films and poured myself a coffee while I waited to be called again. I had a headache, or to be more precise, my brain was ringing with a sort of dull buzzing, like the sound of a blender muffled by a blanket. It was unbearable. At one point I even started to think a blood vessel was going to burst in my brain like it had in my husband's.

Up to that moment, I had wept at my impotence, at my enforced submersions into that ghastly nursing

73

home, at the hideously depressing spectacle inflicted upon me by my mother... But seeing her like that, in her onesie and so out of it as to not even know who she was, had me touching the bottom of the human condition... and it was breathtaking just how far down it was, the bottom.

Terrifying.

And now it was my turn. They were going to find me, coffee in hand, in the break room of the Second District of the DPJ, a trickle of blood running from my ear... My god! The energy required just to live... And my girls would feel exactly the same way when they discovered my body, clutching my cup amidst this ridiculous decor of testosterone-loaded film posters. How depressing it all was.

At some point I was jolted out of my stupor by the sound of loud barking. Platoon and Laser, the two sniffer dogs from the squad, were carrying on at the soft toy animal perched on top of the coffee machine, which they had spotted through the slightly ajar door.

I went out to show it to them to try to quieten them down. They recognised me immediately, going crazy in their excitement, and bringing me back up to the surface.

'They're pretty keen on you, aren't they,' said the dog squad officer, a likeable young fellow with glasses, about thirty years old.

'I adore dogs, but my apartment is too small for me to have any.'

'All a dog needs is to be with its owner; it couldn't care less about the size of the apartment. Laser's going to be looking for a new owner soon. I'll reserve him for you if you want. You two look like you get along well.'

'Isn't he yours?'

'No, the dogs belong to the unit, but once they're nine years old they retire.'

'And what do they do then?'

'If nobody takes them, they're put down.'

All of a sudden, standing there with my fluffy fox terrier under my arm, I was blinded by a shaft of brilliant light. An epiphany in canine form!

'I'll take him right now!'

'I told you, he still has one year to go. But if you want to do a good deed, there's a special refuge for police dogs. You can find it on the internet, on the squad's website.'

'And can you choose… according to their speciality?'

'Their past record is written up under their photo. So, for example, if you have kids, they'll never give you a patrol dog because of its bite.'

'And are they all big like Laser, or are there smaller ones?'

'Generally speaking, they're Belgian Malinois. Look, I'll show you.'

He got out his iPhone and began to scroll through pictures of dogs in cages waiting to be put down.

I wasn't feeling too great as it was… but seeing all those poor creatures looking pleadingly at the lens, well, the dam wall gave way. I couldn't hold back the tears any longer. I was pretty much howling.

'I'm so sorry,' said the cop, totally embarrassed.

'No, no, let's keep looking,' I said, sniffling, 'I'm feeling a bit on edge at the moment. I'd like to see the drug squad dogs, like Laser. They're the most gentle, I'm sure!'

'That one, there, Centaur… Explosives detection.'

'No, no, drugs!' I insisted, between hiccups. I was behaving like a lunatic.

'DNA… that's one ugly-looking mutt! Looks like a kangaroo! *DNA, 9 years old, drugs and currency detection…*'

It was true, he did have a challenging appearance, with his black-and-white-flecked coat, his handle-bar ears and his legs that were too long for his sausage-shaped body. A total mongrel mix of Belgian Malinois, greyhound and some other unidentifiable breed.

But DNA was smiling in the photo, an enthusiastic smile, full of confidence in his future owner.

'Call them, please, maybe they've already killed him or he's about to die this evening!'

'You sure?'

'Yes, yes, I want to adopt that smiling dog. Call them. Now! Tell them I'll come by before they close to collect DNA.'

The poor man took a step backwards, alarmed by my crazed look.

'Listen. My mother is going to die sometime in the next few days. She was taken to a palliative care unit two hours ago for deep sedation. I suspect that means something to you, seeing as you're an animal lover. I've had to put two down so I know what's involved. They look at you when you put them to sleep and they struggle to keep their eyes from closing. And do you know why they do that? So they can take an image of you with them because they love you so much and they know they're not going to see you anymore. Because dogs, you see, they don't believe in God. Dogs are intelligent, not like people... My mother won't even have it as good as a dog does. They'll let her die of hunger – *naturally*, as they say in this backwards country – and I won't be there to hold her hand because it's just too horrible. So, I have to adopt DNA this evening because if I don't, he's going to die, too, and that... that's just not possible. Call them. Please.'

He called.

We went there together and, by the end of that day, 23 July, DNA was home with me.

I loved everything about him: his harlequin coat, the lack of proportion in his body shape which rivalled only mine, his resonant barks that finally drowned out the racket made by my neighbours, and the fact that he instantly decided to attach himself to my feet wherever I went, like a shadow in the shape of a dog.

And my mother completely disappeared from my thoughts.

The moment DNA set foot in my door I had so many things to tell him that I didn't stop talking; it's just that when you haven't had anybody you could really chat to for twenty-five years, there's no shortage of conversation topics.

Plus, we had a job to do as a matter of urgency:

'We're going to take a look on Google Earth to see where that Moroccan idiot could have stashed his load. Yes we are, yes we are, yes we are...'

He stared at me with his moist eyes. *Woof*, he agreed.

Exit 12 on the Janville-Allaine stretch of the A10.

I spent three hours clicking through Street View, which I've had a lot of practice at, seeing as I almost never go on holidays except while seated at my desk on the computer.

I started on the right-hand side of the motorway, which seemed more obvious to me if you were coming from the south.

I imagined Afid panicking, looking for a place to offload the stash, bearing in mind that he had neither the time nor a shovel to dig a hole, and that he was looking for somewhere that would be sheltered from the rain, not knowing when somebody would be able to come and remove his precious cargo. At each junction, I swivelled the arrow through 360 degrees as if looking around. I couldn't see any place where you could discreetly hide a significant quantity of drugs.

For a start, we were in the Beauce region, and the Beauce is as flat as a tack. It's so flat you can spot a single person standing up from a thousand miles around. Anywhere near houses was an impossibility – people are so bored to death in these places that just the sound of a truck is enough to bring them to their windows. All there was within a five-kilometre radius were fields as far as the eye could see, working farms or villages. I didn't find anything except a construction supplies warehouse on the D1183 which was totally fenced off, a tall building housing electricity meters, and a small wooded area. On the D118, there were two other little woods sheltered from view. Nothing else. Even if he had gone further, he would have ended up turning around because he wouldn't have found anything more than I could see. Apart from those few places, everything else was exposed.

The next day then, in crushing heat and feeling overly optimistic, my dog and I set off on a *real life* expedition.

We started at the warehouse, which we approached from behind along a small road. It looked like some type of quarry; the setting for a murder where you expect at any moment to come across a woman spread-eagled on her stomach, her skirt rucked up, her face half submerged in a puddle of water. I let DNA off the lead. Apart from chasing a rabbit, he did nothing but follow me around wagging his tail. We stayed until very late, also exploring all the little surrounding woods, stands of a hundred or so trees clustered around narrow, muddy streams.

As my pretty grey suede shoes disappeared with a sucking noise into the spongy soil, I felt the first twinges of doubt. When I collapsed to the ground after my foot caught in a tree root, I started to curse the world.

I had already wasted four days since Khadija's death; the chances of finding myself face to face with the police or a gang of dealers was increasing with every hour.

What the fuck was I doing there? What if my dog was a dud? Or if Afid was dumber than I thought and had just randomly thrown the drugs into a ditch?

Looking back, I can see that I must have been pretty bloody desperate to have hatched this plan; a bit like the mad woman who buys a lottery ticket in the hope of escaping the bailiffs.

With a little effort, I could at least eliminate one variable: the state of my dog's sense of smell.

Before going home at around two in the morning, we stopped to do a pee at Rue Envierges in the 20th, a street known to be an open-air dope market. No sooner had I opened the car door than DNA shot out like an arrow to go and stick his snout right into the crotch of some black dealer who leaped, terrorised, onto a car bonnet. I whistled. The dog came back to me immediately and we left. So, no problems on that front anyway.

After a few hours' sleep, I drove back to the Beauce, this time adopting a different approach. I went hurtling off the freeway, mimicking Afid's panic, turning at every intersection towards where it seemed from a distance that it might be possible to hide some drugs. I did that four times, each time letting the dog off the leash when I had a good feeling about a place. At one point, we came to a road linking the villages of Janville and Allainville; a lane crossing through a field, lined with huge wind turbines and flanking the A10. In the distance I saw an industrial zone with stacks of pipes and huge piles of gravel and drums. Looking at my iPhone, I realised why I hadn't noticed it on Google Earth – the place where I now was had been hidden by a small cloud just as the satellite had taken the image.

DNA leaped out of the car barking like a lunatic and started indicating the drums and piles of gravel. I saw that the plants bordering the edge of the area were shrivelling up, as if someone had emptied the toxic contents of the barrels over them. Using the handle of my hairbrush as a lever, I popped the cover off one of the drums and... there was the hash, in the form of so-called 'Moroccan bags', giant bricks wrapped in plastic packages with handles. Each one weighing twenty kilos, enough to tear your arm off.

The first barrel I opened had two of them. I tapped the others with a stick, and established they were all full. But there were also one kilo packets of hash hidden under a pile of gravel...

Suddenly I was struck with a sense of the utter recklessness of what I was doing. At a rough guess, there were millions of euros worth of cannabis at the foot of that wind turbine. Every single one of the Benabdelazizes was at risk of being tortured to death for the purpose of producing cute videos aimed at making Afid say where he had stashed the drugs. The police must be holding him in solitary, him and his driver, so that they, the cops, would have a chance of getting there first, otherwise queues would already be forming in this neck of the woods.

For a moment I'd been scared that Afid's sister would go digging through the register of *Les Eoliades* to find my details... But frankly, I had nothing to worry about: if she had even a shred of survival instinct, after the death of her mother she would be hiding in a deep hole somewhere on the outskirts of the *bled*. The only person who might suspect me was Afid himself, and he was in prison.

I started to panic again as I shoved as much as I could into the boot of my car: to be precise, three Moroccan bags and two Ikea bags filled to bursting with bricks of hash.

Once I was back on the motorway, I relaxed. To my surprise, I even started singing at the top of my lungs – *I am a Go Fast, just me, all by myself*, to the tune of Renaud's song *Bande de jeunes* – without realising I was totally stoned. The bricks stank so much despite their cellophane wrapping that when I got back to Paris it was as if I had smoked ten joints. Poor DNA was looking pretty funny too. He was asleep on his back, dribbling litres of drool, the smell of cannabis wafting through to him in his sleep and irritating his nose.

I parked the car in my spot and brought the cannabis – over a hundred kilos of it – up to my apartment as quickly as I could. Then I hired a van and left immediately to go and load up the rest.

I thanked the heavens above that both my girls were on holiday abroad. I also said a prayer of thanks to my disreputable Chinese neighbours, who got up to God knows what sort of funny business – and had even transformed the building's basement at vast expense into a strong room so that they, too, could move between their cellars and their apartments with enormous plastic canvas carry bags. I had actually voted against the works, though I knew it would be purely a matter of form seeing as the Fò family had bought out the entire building. And finally – for the first time – I was grateful for my peasant's constitution. As I scurried along, loaded up on each side with bags weighing twenty kilos, I could feel in my body the generations of indefatigable women who had dragged their kids and their swedes from shtetl to shtetl.

I was very careful at the wind turbine to put everything back the way it had been and to remove any trace of having been there… But then, just as I was turning off the lane and back onto the regional, I saw a convoy of 4x4s appearing out of a cloud of dust and approaching from the other direction. My heart stopped beating for three kilometres at least, until I reached the motorway in one piece.

If I'd left just three minutes later, I'd have been dead and nobody would have had a clue as to why the hell my corpse was even there. The presence of my body in a field in the middle of the Beauce would have been as inexplicable as that of the mythical scuba diver dropped by a Canadair water bomber into a forest fire.

My cellar was stuffed full of my parents' furniture, so I had no choice but to store the hash in my apartment, where you could no longer move without tripping over it. You couldn't breathe either, with the oily, universally recognisable smell of resin pervading the entire place.

I closed the windows and sealed the gap below the front door with my stuffed dachshund draught-excluder, but the smell continued to seep into the stairwell, waging a fratricidal battle with the smell of fish sauce coming from my neighbours. So out I had to go again, this time to buy fifty or so airtight containers. All this on no sleep for the previous 48 hours, and with my back killing me.

In the end, I called two traveller types who came with

their clapped-out truck to empty my cellar of the medieval crap which I still had from my parents. While they were busy loading their vehicle with marvels such as the famous helmet-turned-lamp as well as a series of tapestries depicting the Siege of Orleans and some furniture à la Spanish Inquisition – which they seemed to find unfathomably beautiful – I surreptitiously removed my father's short-barrelled.357 Magnum.

I had been planning to get rid of that revolver – not only because I find weapons hideously ugly, but because this particular one had killed people whose bodies had been buried on *The Estate*. After all, if one day somebody stumbled upon those remains, it would inevitably lead back to me; and then if they were to find the weapon that had been used to bump off all those people, I would find myself having to offer all sorts of exhausting explanations. But getting rid of a gun is the sort of job you never get around to doing, always putting it off to tomorrow.

On that memorable day, when I emptied my cellar so I could use it to store my hash, I finally decided to keep it.

With the cold weight of the metal in my hand, I thought about how you never remember what you felt about the events you witnessed as a child, almost as if they were made-up stories that had happened to somebody else.

One image comes back to me often: of my father, standing motionless for several long minutes in the middle of the lawn. To the untrained eye, he was merely admiring his garden. His cauliflower-sized roses that neither I nor my mother were allowed to cut. His irises every colour of the rainbow. The wisteria that climbed all over his bench; his hedges trimmed into round balls; his pyramid-shaped yews… But that wasn't at all what he was looking at; he was occupied by something much further removed in time and space – the valley of the Medjerda river where he had grown up.

It had driven him crazy to be torn from his roots without having a chance to fight for his Tunisian farm.

There in the middle of *The Estate*, under a weeping willow, he had installed a reproduction of one of Emile Boisseau's allegorical sculptures, *Defence of the Home*. For those who don't know, it's a sculpture in the *art pompier* tradition dating from 1887, the original of which stands in the Square d'Ajaccio in the 7th arrondissement of Paris. It was reproduced in a series of different metals, and we had the cheap version in zinc and antimony at our place.

No work of art better expressed the mental image my father had of himself. Just like the valorous Gaul clad in a simple fur skin, protecting his wife and infant with his broken sword, he would die defending his family and *The Estate*, weapons in hand. *Perit sed in armis*.

When night fell, the tall street-lights along the motorway illuminated the garden like an Expressionist film set – especially when the elongated silhouette of a burglar could be seen slipping through the rustling shadows cast by the tall trees. On two occasions, I saw somebody scale the wall, make their way around the house and, after seeing that the place was both occupied and impregnable, leave again the same way they had arrived.

But one time, in the middle of the night, one of these miscreants went a step too far, carrying off *Defence of the Home* after crudely knocking it from its plinth with a chisel.

The next day, unable to bear this wound to his narcissism, my father bought the notorious .357 Magnum from one of his spook friends, complete with silencer so he could shoot intruders without waking us up. He killed the first one when I was eight years old, and buried him at the bottom of the garden, in the place where we burned the dead leaves in autumn. I remember firing a few questions at my father that day, having spotted him crossing the lawn at high speed with a body falling over the edge of a wheelbarrow. He replied that if these guys didn't want to be shot, all they had to do was not break into *The Estate* after nightfall – because he had the law on his side. It was called legitimate self-defence. And anyway, no colonial settler who ever lived in a house surrounded by walls would behave any differently.

I don't know how many he killed in all, because generally it happened at night, and at a time in my life when I wasn't paying too much attention to things, but I do know there's a veritable mass grave down there in the leaf-covered pit. It was our poor manservant who assumed the onerous task of burying the bodies – he told me himself one day, after asking me to come with him to the pharmacy to buy a girdle for his back. What's more, my father must have lent his pit to others or used it for activities related to Mondiale, because when I cleared out the house after he'd died, I found twenty odd identity cards in a shoe box. All men aged between twenty and forty years old. I put them in an envelope addressed to the local police station which produced not the slightest consequence, not even a brief article in the newspapers.

During the time my parents lived there, *The Estate* was like a giant clam whose shell, from time to time, would close over some nameless fish in the silence of the ocean.

When my father died, my mother swiftly sold it and everything in it for next to nothing. The guy who bought it was an arrogant arsehole – a despot for whom *The Estate* was the perfect cover for his villainous tyranny over the family he would keep confined behind the walls and isolated by the deafening noise of the motorway. While signing the contract, he threw a salacious glance at his three daughters and confided that he had been quite taken by the place… They were choice recruits – I'd sensed it as soon as I set eyes on them – for the *People of the Road*.

Not so long ago, I drove by and climbed onto the bonnet of my car to look over the wall. The necropolis has been planted over. But if you were to fly over the garden at low altitude, you would notice immediately that the plants there are abnormally green; the sort of green that indicates soil bloated with phosphates.

I must have been fifteen, the last time I saw the .357 Magnum in action.

In addition to being located alongside the road of death, *The Estate* was bordered on the other side by the Presidential hunting grounds, from which it was separated by a mere wire mesh fence. Whenever France sent its Ministers and their guests on an excursion to kill some innocent animals in an attempt to assert its identity as a big-swinging-dick of a country, said innocent animals used to run to our place for cover at the first sound of a shot fired. So the garden would be strewn with fifty or so pheasants and partridges; fat, over-nourished birds taunting the hunters from our green lawn. The beaters would do their best to recover them, but every time they tried to gain access, they were always met with the same flat-out rejection from my father.

But one Sunday, on the occasion of a visit by an African potentate, the situation turned to tragedy.

In order to entertain French Africa, a military truck filled with hapless deer had been brought from Chambord so they could be released into the forest. One of them had given the hunters the slip and had leaped over the wire fence to seek refuge under our sun porch. This time, the beaters didn't ring on the door politely but invaded *The Estate*, cutting through the wire. The potentate and his courtiers followed, all done up like the subjects in that 19th-century painting *King Maximilian II of Bavaria returning from the hunt*, their hats adorned with a pheasant's plume.

My father rushed out like a Fury, brandishing his Magnum – but realising he couldn't get away with shooting anybody, he took aim at the head of the deer, which exploded as he shot it at point-blank range, splattering the black king's pretty tweed outfit with blood.

French Africa departed *The Estate* very disgruntled; my father had ruined his day.

*

I knew how to use the Magnum. My father, good colonial that he was, had taught me at the same age he himself had learned, that's to say, at the age of ten. I still remembered the recoil ripping into my shoulder as he made me shoot, over and over, until I could absorb the shock with my body. So when my parents went out to a restaurant, they could leave me alone between the motorway and the forest with the revolver on my bedside table and not waste a moment worrying whether or not I might be scared – after all, what baby-sitter could be as good as a .357 Magnum?

Now my old companion was resuming its place at my side. Just in case.

It had taken me two days and a night to transfer the drugs from the wind turbines to my place.

I understood why Khadija had used the term *little fish* when she had spoken with her son on the telephone: the Benabdelaziz's trademark was two fish, drawn head-to-tail, yin and yang, branded into their resin. But that was only the loose bricks I had found stashed into the pile of gravel. The rest – the Moroccan bags – belonged to the other families she'd told me about. Other *tags*, to use the lingo, were thermo-engraved onto the bricks. A third were branded with the Audi logo, with four interlocking circles; others with the number 10, in the style of some hot-shot dude's team football shirt; and others had some bizarre symbol that looked like a pentagon.

Before closing my cellar door, I stepped back to admire my organisational handiwork: there in the cellar were 1.2 tonnes of cannabis. One thousand two hundred kilos of top-quality *frappe*, at 5,000 euros a kilo. I hardly dared do the sums I was so overcome by my audacity. I had shifted 1.2 tonnes on my own back. Fifty-two Moroccan bags, each weighing twenty kilos, two per airtight container that I had filled one at a time, stacking them up as I went, as well as one hundred and sixty loose one kilo blocks. I had even thought of a little step ladder.

Completely exhausted, I dropped in to the geriatric intensive care unit at the hospital to see how things were with my mother.

In the corridor off her room, I came across the inevitable families bivouacking under the fluoro lights with thermos flasks, blankets and Candy Crush, no use to anyone but there because… well, because they had to be there, didn't they, so that whatever happened they didn't miss the last wheeze of the Ancient One.

The manager of the unit, a woman as neat as she was disagreeable, and an absolute dead-ringer for Nurse Ratched in *One Flew Over the Cuckoo's Nest*, received me, explaining what was likely to happen in the coming days.

'Your mum is not yet terminal…'

'I think you're mistaken there! In fact, it's been quite some time now that she's been terminal, that she's been suffering and all you've done is stuff her full of sedatives,' I replied bitterly.

'She's able to swallow again, and so apart from the

macular degeneration, she's not suffering from any other illness. She hasn't got any bedsores and her bloods are like those of a young woman…'

'There's nothing left of her mind and even less hope for any improvement… and her back is in agony as a result of her being confined to her bed!'

'We've done another scan, and the bleeding which was apparent in her left hemisphere is now in the process of being reabsorbed. I think she's going to be able to make a slow recovery to her previous condition.'

'Previous to what? This is grotesque! She's in pain, do you hear me! She's been suffering like a dog now for two and a half years. The director of the nursing home assured me you would be putting her under continuous deep sedation…'

'Listen, your mum…'

'Please! Stop saying *mum* as if I were seven years old. I can't stand it any more! Everybody has been talking to me about *my mum* since the start of this nightmare… One day I'd like somebody to explain to me this idiotic practice. You're all doing it, so it must be what you're all taught at college, right? What's the idea? To infantilise people so that whatever happens they don't suffocate *mum* with a cushion.'

I felt utterly outraged by this woman, this intermediary of death, knowing all the while that my indignation would crash headlong into a brick wall. And, sure enough, she continued in exactly the same tone.

'Two days ago, your mum had problems swallowing; that's no longer the case. If that had continued, we would have had to consider whether to insert a feeding tube. Artificial nutrition is a form of treatment and the law authorises stopping treatments. Your mum has started eating again without any issues, so she has evidently not decided to die.'

'You don't have the right to let people who have deteriorated to this point continue to live! She's completely delirious, she's blind, she's bedridden and since this most recent stroke, she has been living – and when I say living, I'm weighing my words carefully – she has been living in utter terror every second of the day.'

'Your mum survived the camps...'

'And?'

'Our ethical duties require us to recognise our patients' wishes to the extent we're able, even if they themselves are not in a position to formulate those wishes expressly. I think that when you have survived such testing circumstances, it is inconceivable that you would give up the will to live. I myself would have opted for the feeding tube.'

'*You* would have opted...! What do you know about what she thinks? Are you a member of one of those bullshit religious groups or something – the Society of Saint Pius X, is that it? And I just have to suck it up?'

She made a gesture with her hand to indicate the matter was closed.

'We're going to keep her here under observation for a few days to allow her to regain a degree of comfort, and if she continues to eat as she is now, she'll return to the nursing home.'

I was speechless.

Then she added in a glacial monotone: 'We're not here to put people down, Madame. If anybody is suffering here, it's you.'

As to that last point, she was right.

I went home, went to bed and slept for twenty hours.

Two days later, flicking through *Le Parisien* with my croissant and coffee at the local café, I read an article that both saddened me and filled me with relief: the previous day an inmate by the name of Afid B. had had his throat slit at Villepinte prison.

Most women spend their life trying to extricate themselves from the example set by their mother... There was no getting around the fact that I was doing exactly the opposite. In fact, I was going even further. I was remaking myself in the image my own mother used to hold up as her ideal: the intrepid Jewish woman.

4

You snooze, you lose

It was the end of July. The sun was scorching the sky. The Parisians were migrating south to the beaches. And just as I was getting started in my new career, Philippe, my cop fiancé, took up his position as Commander of the drug squad for the Second District DPJ.

'We'll see each other more this way,' he'd said cheerfully, when he'd announced the news two months earlier, on the day of his appointment.

I was genuinely happy for him – but back then, I was only a simple court translator-interpreter and I didn't yet have 1.2 tonnes of hash in my basement.

Philippe.

So, he's a man. Broad-backed, muscly, carrying a bit of extra weight, big, beautiful hands. A kind face with a thick head of hair, a rare thing at fifty-eight. The sort of guy everyone wants to please, who can be measured by his generosity, by the number of friends he has, or the number of godchildren – by everything, really... A guy whose social standing was plain for all to see at significant occasions such as birthdays or leaving drinks. A guy whose funeral would mean a graveyard crowded with mourners.

Physically, I couldn't say whether he was my type. In any event, he looked nothing like the only man who had ever really meant anything to me, namely, my husband, whom people always assumed was my big brother, we looked so alike. In fact, prior to Philippe, I hadn't ever really experienced physical otherness. I'm not saying I'd lived like a nun for twenty years, but my sex life had been limited to one-night stands, always with criminal lawyers, by definition a bunch of lying, unfaithful, narcissistic womanisers… And this was when I still belonged to the *Milf* category – *mother I'd like to fuck*. Once I hit forty, it was all over.

It was Philippe's desire for me that really won out; a desire that was strong and genuine, that shone in his eyes when he looked at me, and that would have carried away any menopausal creature…

I loved having him around – who wouldn't have? – because as well as being integrity personified, he was intelligent, cultured and witty. By combining my life with his, I told myself at the time, a bit of his solidity might perhaps rub off on me. But when he was with me, or worse, on top of me, I felt as if I was being swallowed up, both literally and figuratively, without knowing if I even liked it. Sure, he was a considerate lover of whom I could ask anything and who was able to make me come for hours at a time… but after enquiring whether

I was completely satisfied, he would snuggle up against me, bury his face in my neck and slip blissfully into a peaceful and grateful sleep. And then, with his body like a dead horse cutting off my circulation and killing my back, and his deep, hot breath condensing on my skin… how can I say this… I had only one wish, and that was for him to leave. One time I stayed the night at his place and I didn't get a wink of sleep the whole night. The colours at his place, his carpet, everything… In short, I would have the taste of congealed fat in my mouth until he turned off the light. If he hadn't had custody of his son, I think he would have suggested we live together… and what would I have said? Especially since he was ready to make all sorts of concessions. I could have said: *I'm sorry, but I don't like having somebody stuck to my back when I'm sleeping.* Or: *The decor at your place makes me feel like throwing up.* And he would have agreed to change to make me happy because he was in love. Not just the way you can be when you're 58 years old, facing the terror of growing old alone – no, he loved me with enthusiasm and kindness. And me? From time to time, when I was swept up by one of those waves of despondency to which I was prone, it comforted me to feel the warmth of his body, the beating of his heart. Like an animal. But to go from that to thinking about him when he wasn't there, to waiting impatiently for him, to holding his hand, just like that, for the pleasure of touching him? No!

We would see each other when our schedules permitted, so that we had the feeling of being short-changed, of not having the time to really get to know the other's personality or their faults. And while I had plenty of faults, *he* had one big one: he believed in God. Philippe, this man who was integrity personified, intelligent, cultured and witty… believed in God! It just seems so unlikely that anybody could give any credibility to such a load of rubbish. He could have confided in me a belief that our fate as humans was pre-determined by a dish of celestial noodles, and I would have found it less ridiculous.

One day, when I was taking my daughters to the Natural History Museum, I remember seeing a couple of Saudi tourists: a woman in a *niqab* accompanied by her husband. At the time, there was a lot of talk of creationism in the United States and you'd often come across nonsense like the fact that dinosaurs disappeared because they were too heavy to climb onto Noah's Ark.

I'm an Arabic translator, and therefore supposed to know everything about Arabs, the religion included – you should know that in Arabic, there's hardly a sentence without a reference to Allah – so I couldn't resist approaching this rather unusual couple to enquire as to the precise Islamic view of dinosaurs. You got the feeling the guy didn't know quite what to think of these immense creatures. He introduced himself as a professor of theology at the Sharia College in Riyadh. After some time reflecting, all the while stroking his beard, he told me with a learned air that there were some verses in the Quran that spoke of the creation of the universe in six days, but that the length of the days was not clearly specified, given that the sun, the stars… all of those things…

weren't really set up, and therefore there was nothing stopping you from envisaging days that were several million years long. The resulting ambiguity accordingly left open the possibility of a very old Earth populated by these huge animals. But to go from there to saying that man was descended from apes or from a bacteria, as suggested by the frescoes at the entrance to the museum: well, that was the stuff of infidels! He finished by inviting me to undertake my Hijrah – that is, to leave France to go and live a wholesome Islamic life in a holy land where such ridiculous notions were not taught.

Philippe more or less believed the same thing about evolution as that man who had walked straight out of the Middle Ages, and yet he was ready to wage war against him in the name of civilisation. In short, I'm not sure what to do with a belief in God except see it as some form of mental disorder...

The first customers of my new life were served up to me on a platter by the drug squad case involving three Moroccans which I happened to be working on at the Second District DPJ. It was the perfect convergence. All the stars were aligned: here was a bunch of guys sufficiently idiotic not to wonder where I might have sprung from, and who had an urgent need for product as a result of a *delivery mishap*.

I always take great care in my work to translate word for word. That's my trademark. I don't miss a scrap of what I'm listening to, and when I'm transcribing I set out to convey the tone and style of conversations so as to maximise reading pleasure. And on this point I confess to a shamefully patrician and perverse fascination with stupidity:

Intercept No. 7235 dated Thursday, 25 July. Intercept taken from the telephone device of the person under surveillance originating from line no. 2126456584539, the registered owner of which is not known to the Moroccan authorities. The person using the line is Karim Moufti alias Scotch. His interlocutor is Akim Boualem alias Chocapic.

Words in Arabic have been translated by Madame Patience Portefeux who has been engaged for this purpose and who hereby jointly certifies this transcript.

Scotch: *Don't start giving me some crap about me being in shit 'cos it was you put me in it, and you're in the same shit yourself. Words like that, bro', I can take it from some nobody I don't know but not comin' from you. Every night I'm goin' to the hookah bar and you're tellin' me: Don' stress man, s'all good, don' stress… And here I am bro', here I find myself with some stuff that's been dunked in petrol. Camel shit that stinks so much of petrol you could light it up with a match. I couldn't even give that shit away, that's how much they don't want it. Hamdullah, if you think you can manage to get your notes back at your end, go ahead bro – and I'm telling you, good luck with that – but don't ask me to pay for crap in that state… That shit is just trash, man.*

Chocapic: *I'm gonna take my notes straight back outta his sonuvabitch hands. I don't want no more from that* *motherfucker. I don't want nothin' no more, even if he comes back to me. Don't wanna hear nothin' more from him!*

Scotch: *He's shoved a big fat finger up your ass and you ain't ever gonna see another cent. You gotta show no mercy! Action reaction!*

Chocapic: *It's makin' me sick, man. I'm not sleepin'. I'm not eatin'. I'm not breathin'. He's gone disappeared with my 180 big ones for a metre of crap… He did me with the photo… You feel me, huh?*

Scotch: *I can see that, sure, I can see that, but your problem, man, is that you're too sure of yourself. 'Don't stress man, s'all good, don' stress, I got this…' This is what you get, bro' that's why you're sitting here like the world's own ass-hole. But I gotta deliver, no matter what! And I got nothin' to go down. I swear on the Quran, it's breakin' my balls. I'm the one left with the responsibility, and that's stressin' me, bro'.*

The key to drug-dealing is consistency. You have to guarantee an uninterrupted supply of the product at all costs because the customer is fickle and always in a hurry. If a dealer can't supply anymore, within a week, the goodwill value of his book of phone numbers plummets – we're talking here about thousands of euros. A shortage of product is the dealer's chronic sickness. It's a bit like in the singing business: lots of talented performers, and barely any decent stuff to sing. To make sure you have work, ideally you want to write, compose and sing – to plant, transport and sell.

So, you can understand the distress of the cretin-in-chief known as Scotch who's got nothing left in the shop except cannabis that's going to be shoved right back in his face – and at the height of summer, what's more, when everybody's heading to the beaches with something to smoke in their bag.

The ill fortune of his supplier, Chocapic, therefore puts him in a seriously awkward position.

This latter accepted a delivery in the belief that it would comply with the sample, but a leak in the *Go Fast* car had spoiled the whole load, making it taste like petrol. The unfortunate Chocapic has paid out 180 big ones for one metre – that's to say 180,000 euros for one hundred kilos – with no hope of any return because his 'business partner' Scotch is refusing the delivery, which doesn't meet the standard he was entitled to expect.

Taking into account the wholesaler's margin, I had worked out that Scotch must have at his disposal 200,000 euros of liquid assets, and that what was on offer from Chocapic must be very poor quality Pakistani product.

I went down to the phone shop on the street outside my apartment and bought a pre-paid calling card so I could contact this Scotch by SMS. Hoping the fool could read Arabic, I wrote:

> Due to recent delivery am selling half metre of quality at 250. Check photo.

> (50kg of quality hash at 250,000 euros. Check sample.)

The next day the Second District DPJ sent me, amongst other translations, my own SMS as well as his reply and the rest of our exchange.

How strange to be confronted with your own words. It's like being on a balcony, watching yourself walk down the street, and walking down the street at the same time.

When I had sent that message two days earlier, Scotch had replied straight away: OK.

I'd followed quickly with: Contact Fleury Quick, today, 17h00. With photo.

It wasn't a random decision, choosing the Fleury Quick halal fast food joint as the setting for the deal. Anything is possible in that tiny fast-food place, situated at the intersection between the main road into Paris and Rue des Peupliers, which runs past the biggest prison in Europe. Inmates' families rub shoulders with their drug-dealing mates and the permanently broke Muslim prison staff. I used to eat there back when I was translating Disciplinary Committee proceedings inside the prison, and I remembered well its vipers' nest feel: it was ugly, dirty, and insanely busy.

Before showing up at my business meeting, I obviously had to change my look. Most importantly, I had to hide my white hair which stood out in a crowd of thousands.

I had great fun disguising myself. I opted for Moroccan *bled* chic: fake black and gold Chanel sunglasses, leopard print hijab, black khôl eyeliner, pantsuit with long tunic, gold bracelets (lots of them) and diamanté watch, orange nails and shiny nylons. I was unrecognisable. A very respectable Maghrebi business woman. The perfect chameleon.

I hailed a taxi to take me there and told him to wait for me.

I recognised my contacts as soon as I arrived.

A joy to behold.

Porsche Cayenne with tinted windows parked in a disabled parking spot and surrounded by discarded fast-food wrappers. Rap music and air-con blasting, doors open. They were fat bastards with stringy chin-strap beards minus the moustache, cropped pants, flip-flops, Fly Emirates Paris Saint Germain T-shirts accentuating rolls of lard. To top it off, a dash or two of summer-chic accessorising: a Louis Vuitton clutch resting on the paunch along with Tony Montana mirrored sunnies.

The complete look. The new orientalism.

'Hello, I'm Madame Ben Barka. I'm the one who contacted you. I've got some product that comes from the *bled* and I heard through one of your customers that you've got issues with your supplier.'

The three of them looked at me as if they were hallucinating; the last thing they had expected was to have to do a deal with their mother.

'Who…?'

'I told you, my name is Madame Ben Barka, and I've got some good quality stuff from down there to sell.'

Silence. My face is impenetrable. My eyes immobile behind my branded sunglasses.

'Oh really?' said the fat one with the PSG T-shirt at last, full of himself – Karim Moufti alias Scotch, whom I recognised by his moronic intonation.

I pulled a 100-gram sample out of my handbag.

'Here's the photo. It's 4,500 euros a kilo, top quality, but I'll do you a deal if you take more than 50. I'll do you an even better deal if you take more than that.'

'How much is more?' Scotch asked me, handling his sample of hash as if it were a dead octopus.

The Mouftis and their mates were born in France and knew nothing about the *bled* except its beaches. Moroccans raised far from their native soil, their roots exposed; hydroponic Moroccans. They could just about sprinkle their speech with the odd Arabic phrase, but carrying on an actual conversation was completely beyond them. Scotch was looking at me intently, moving his lips in sync as I spoke. You got the feeling from his eyes – their pupils dilated by the fumes coming out of his head – that it was pretty hot work in that brain of his.

'We can start at 50 for 225 which comes to 4,500 a kilo, which is the Spanish price for quality like this. Transportation to France is on me, but 50 is the minimum you've got to take. If you sell it at 10 for 60, that already gives you a margin of 75,000. I don't work with a *saraf* so I want the money direct and if there's a single note missing, it's the last time I work with you. That's the deal. You've got my number.'

'How much is more?' asked Scotch again, completely hypnotised.

How did he manage to look so damned stupid!

'More means more. Much more. But first let's see if we can all work nicely together, and then we'll think about it.'

As I left in my taxi, I looked in the rear-view mirror.

The three of them hadn't moved, still standing there stiff as boards in their flip-flops.

The translations I did next were enough to warm the heart. It's nice to know you've got a good product.

Intercept No. 7432 dated Tuesday, 3 August. Intercept taken from the telephone device of the person under surveillance originating from line no. 2126456584539 the registered owner of which is not known to the Moroccan authorities. The person using the line is Karim Moufti alias Scotch. His interlocutor is Mounir Charkani alias Lizard.
Words in Arabic translated by Madame Patience Portefeux who has been engaged for this purpose and who hereby jointly certifies this transcript.

Scotch: *On my mother's life, I'm telling you, it's the OG shit, totally sick. It's got the earth in it from the bled, you can smell it, it's so damned sick, you got grasshoppers hopping around on your head. It's the country, man... (Laughter.)*
Lizard: *You've smoked too much, bro'.*
Scotch: *Dude, bring it on, I'm gonna work the whole year with this weird-ass godmother chick. Not even thinking if she might be a cop... It's such good shit I'm gonna do it for you for 8.*
Lizard: *You can't resist farting above your arsehole man. (Laughter.) Let's see it. I wanna show a photo like that to my cousin with the wheels.*
Scotch: *You know what fuckin' Brandon said, about the 12 I showed him in the photo... He didn't fuck around. 'Your*

juice, it's hot shit, I'm gonna put in an order straight up, one hundred percent,' that's what he said…

Lizard: *Dude…*

Scotch: *Kill two stones with one bird, with your cousin, bro'. The Tunisian. Things are movin' in the city. We'll have a hookah at the Prince and have a meeting, 'cos dude, I'm feelin' it, one hundred percent. You can start sayin' to them already to get their notes together for a metre, I'm tellin' you.*

I was forced to leave the word *godmother* in the transcript, because it appeared in French in the text that had been submitted to me. It bothered me at the time, but then I told myself that I'd just found my criminal alias. So, I'd be the *Godmother*. I imagined the crime squad detectives already had me down by that name in the numerous exchanges in French that didn't pass through my filter. There was a lot of chatter going around about my hash; it wasn't every day that such good quality product fell into the lap of dealers quite so eager to get their hands on it.

I thought about where the transactions could take place. It had to be somewhere both discreet and safe, but also where there would be enough people around for me to feel secure. After all, I didn't want my customers to hold me up at gun point and take back the money they'd just handed over to me – best-case scenario – or, even worse, to torture a confession out of me as to where I'd stashed the rest of the drugs. A place where you could give big bags to Arabs without attracting the attention of one of the thousands of patrol cars criss-crossing greater Paris thanks to the state of emergency... The Quick fast food joint parking lot was small, and thus too exposed, so I opted for the Fleury prison parking lot, where the families of the inmates are always coming and going, laden with bags. It might seem an odd place to deal drugs, but there's no better place to get swallowed up in a crowd.

I put my two plastic checked bags from the Tati store, weighing 25kg each, on trolleys to avoid doing my back in, then loaded them into my car in the parking space under my apartment building. I drove to another arrondissement, parked, and got a taxi to take me and the bags to Fleury. There, I asked the driver to wait for me on the edge of the great expanse of carpark, with the two bags in his boot, while I looked for my so-called nephews who weren't answering their phones.

I walked over to the Cayenne parked on the other side of the carpark. Breathe, concentrate. As a child, I'd learned how to cross borders with an 'unaccompanied minor' sign around my neck, and my pink down puffer jacket stuffed full of five-hundred-franc notes. The secret is to submit control of every molecule in your body to your mind. It's like a bike, you don't forget how to ride it, and not everybody can do it.

I got into the car with the smoky windows and took out a battery-operated bank note counter. The problem was that there was a huge amount of 10s and 20s and it would have taken hours to get through them.

'I don't take small denominations!'

'Money's money,' said Scotch, annoyed, in Arabic.

There was something about his tone I supremely

disliked. An underlying threat, something like *you'll take my dough, you filthy bitch* – and I can't stand that with men, especially fat bastards weighing 110 kilos who clench their fists when they're irritated. It just makes me want to humiliate them.

'10s, 20s, 50s… that's small-time loser crap. The smallest I take is a 100. Tell me right now if you're a loser so I don't have to waste my time.'

I let the word *loser* slide from my lips in French with a Moroccan accent you could cut with a knife. It was magnificent.

The problem for dealers is that 10s and 20s are the currency on the streets, and they quickly turn into mountains of bank notes. These then have to be exchanged for large denominations, and that can only be done by way of a laundering system. By calling Scotch a *loser*, I had reduced him to a street dealer, when in his dreams he was Tony Montana. What's more, my request would reduce his margin, forcing him to spend an extra 10 euros for every 100 euro note.

'OK, I've got 112,500 here,' I said, 'which means you only get one of the two bags. Just this once, I'll accept five hundred 50s, but it's the last time. That other stuff is just bullshit.'

'We wanna count the shit.'

'No problem. Just so you know, I also do bags of 20 for the wholesale market… It's more practical. If you want to count… Hey, you…'

I pointed to the one who had to be Mohamed Moufti, alias Momo, Scotch's little brother.

I'd bet my life on my taxi driver having at least one brother in prison. I say that because on our way there, he'd used the term *incarceration*. I pay careful attention to words – it's my job – and you only say that word out loud if you work in the law or if you're involved with the law…

In any case, the driver saw nothing unusual about a young Moroccan guy helping his mother with her laundry bags in a place where everybody is carrying large checked plastic bags filled with washing. Once he was back in his seat after removing one of the two bags from the boot, I opened it up as if I was just checking to see what was in it, and showed Scotch's brother the 25 neatly stacked one kilo packets. The transaction was swiftly completed and everybody went their own way.

'What if I find the notes for another metre before the 15th?' Scotch asked me over the phone once I was back in the taxi.

'I'll do it for 4 for a metre and a half, 100s and 200s only though, otherwise you get nothing,' I said, not beating around the bush, and thinking how I'd be translating the exchange the next day.

Needless to say, the party Philippe had organised that very evening to celebrate his new position could not have come at a worse time. After my own private celebration for having made it home alive to walk the dog and finger my one hundred and twelve thousand euros, I then had to put on my game face and get myself to a café in the 20th arrondissement packed to the rafters with cops. I was not in the best of moods.

When I arrived, he was surrounded by male and female colleagues, all chatting away while inelegantly quaffing their beer straight from the bottle. I helped myself to a – I'm not sure what it was, something white, warm, alcoholic and bubbly – then planted myself in a corner waiting for it to end.

It's not that I'm particularly snobby, they just don't make me laugh anymore, all those cops, with their dodgy jokes that I know off by heart. Also, I don't like drinking cheap plonk. Before things got a bit *tight,* as they say, if anybody had asked me whether I liked champagne, I wouldn't have known what to say. It was part of my natural habitat, what had always been poured into my nonchalantly held-out glass. But after twenty-five years of unlikely drinks parties with all kinds of concoctions on offer – all of them white, bubbly and utterly revolting – one thing I have worked out is that champagne has nothing to do with all that shit. So there you go.

I could feel Philippe's eyes riveted on me and it was making me uncomfortable.

'What?' I said, almost aggressively.

'Nothing,' came his answer. 'I'm just looking at you. It's not every day I get the chance. I'm making the most of it.' His eyes were shining with tenderness. 'Damn, you're quite the paradox, aren't you. You always lower your eyes whenever anybody speaks to you, like you're shy, but at the same time you're giving off this feeling of kick-ass confidence – like the very worst scum bags in fact.'

I internally acknowledged his perceptiveness, making a mental note to be a little more open in future – without carrying on like some character in *Crime and Punishment*, obviously.

'And that's a compliment, I suppose.'

He smiled sweetly: 'Of course, because compliments are all I have for you… You still haven't told me how you really learnt Arabic.'

'I've told you plenty of times. I've got a gift for languages and I studied it!'

'Can you believe that yesterday, one of the Moroccans I was interviewing about the murder of that young dealer specifically asked for you, *in personam*… He wouldn't take no for an answer – he had to have you, only you! According to him, you translate better than anyone else.'

'What murder? Which young guy? Which Moroccan? I don't know what you're talking about!'

And it was true, at the time, I had no idea what he was referring to, when suddenly the driver who had come up from the *bled* together with Afid Benabdelaziz popped back into my head. I'd forgotten all about him.

'It wasn't that long ago, you know, when those drug dealers were arrested on 14 July… Even I'm up to speed and I didn't even have the job at that point…'

'Yes, yes, so much has happened in the meantime… my mother… the hospital…'

'The dog…'

'Yes, the dog, too!'

'It's a good thing, what you've done for that poor creature… If you need a hand looking after it, I'm around!'

'I really love him.'

'One of the dealer guys had his throat slit in prison.'

'How was I supposed to know that?'

'You could have read about it in the papers!'

'In *Le Monde diplomatique*?'

He laughs.

'In all the papers, except *Le Monde diplo*. For sure it's a settling of scores because a week before, his mother was attacked outside her place. We haven't been able to find out anything more because she died of a heart attack.'

'Yes, yes, I remember – the Moroccans who dumped their load on their way up from Spain… Somebody must have recovered the drugs by now.'

'Probably, but something's telling me it's not the rightful owners. There's a lot of chatter about it out there, especially that they were transporting it for other people… Anyway, to cut a long story short, the driver was saying nothing.

'So, what ended up happening…?'

The driver… Shit… What did he want from me?

'He went back to his cell. The investigating magistrate will question him again. We've got time. Remember, criminal proceedings have been started, which means they can be held in pre-trial detention for a year, so nobody's in any hurry. They'll call you. I've put a note in the file… So, you didn't answer me, where did you learn Arabic?'

'Well, my nanny taught me to speak it between the ages of six and seventeen. After that, I studied it.'

'My son had an Algerian babysitter too. She used talk to him in Arabic so he still knows a few words. But that's a far cry from being able to speak it fluently.'

'Well, my nanny was a man, and he didn't just babysit me, he raised me.'

'Really?'

'Yes, a man.'

'So what was his name, this nanny?'

'Bouchta.'

I had not said that name for a very, very long time. Not out loud anyway, because sometimes I would call it out in my sleep if I was having a bad dream. Curiously, now this whole episode is behind me, I don't do that anymore, but at the time, after twenty-five years of lethargy, while I was in the process of resuming my position in the Mafioso continuum of my family, my brain was behaving like an old sponge. If I squeezed it, a flood of memories would emerge...

Bouchta...

Oh, my Bouchta... my dear Bouchta.

A mediocre homemaker at best, my mother did absolutely nothing around the house, and certainly didn't do any cleaning. My father didn't hold it against her, quite the contrary: the wife of a pied-noir upon whom fortune has smiled should not have to ruin her finger-nails scrubbing pots and pans. On the other hand, she ought to know how to manage her staff – which she didn't do either. If I had to sketch a timeline of my younger childhood years, it would consist of a succession of maids, scoldings, accusations of breakages or theft and slammed doors. In the end, exasperated by the permanent state of chaos that reigned in our house – whether it was the Portuguese woman loathed by our Doberman, the deaf Polish woman, or the slob from the Creuse – my father decided to settle our domestic affairs once and for all, and left for Tunisia to buy Bouchta.

His previous owner was one of his old colonial friends who had stayed in the *bled* after Independence. This guy still practised *khemmessat*, a type of medieval serfdom consisting of attaching a man to a bit of land by way of an inextinguishable debt. My father must have had to pay a lot to buy off said debt, since he used to complain to all his old Tunisian friends living in France that his *Arab had cost him a pretty penny…* The wives of these colonials, nostalgic for the Moorish women they had left behind, would turn green with envy at the luxury in which my mother basked; not only did she own electrical appliances, she also had a slave to use them.

Bouchta didn't work the land but instead took care of the housework and the cooking. He was what Malcolm X used to call the *house Negro* insofar as he accepted the authority of the Whites as the natural order. I simply can't see any other explanation for the fact he didn't murder us all, dog included, in our sleep after one too many exclamations of *Bouchta, asba!* on the part of my father; *asba* being the most vulgar expression you can imagine in Arabic – something along the lines of *my cock up your mother's ass* – and universally used by the colonials to punctuate their speech.

Bouchta, asba, the soup! Asba, fissa, the cheese!

As to the question of poor Bouchta's membership of the human species (and that of Arabs in general) my parents were, for once, in agreement.

In my father's racial hierarchy – which had room for anti-Jewish, anti-Maltese, anti-Italian, even anti-pied-noir sentiment – and at the summit of which, as a *Tunisian* colonial, he put himself, Arabs had no place whatsoever. How could they? According to this scheme, Arabs were not people, but inconvenient and rebellious pieces of farming machinery. They were known as *burnous*, after their traditional hooded garments, evoking an image of flesh sweating away underneath as the maximum amount of juice was extracted.

At last, thanks to Bouchta's presence and the power of the imagination to fuse two utterly different places, *The Estate* became Tunisia, just as for Marguerite Duras the river Seine became the Mekong.

My father would joyfully bellow abuse in his nursery Arabic to his new plaything, whom he had dressed up as Nestor from Tintin in a striped waist-coat and bow tie. He had planted a fig tree, and – despite his lower back problems – would sit perched atop an oriental pouf while listening to Lili Boniche and Reinette l'Oranaise, favourites from his colonial youth.

For dinner, there would be roasted capsicums in oil and chicken with olives, with strudel for dessert – a sign of Austria's continuing resistance to Tunisian hegemony.

The first time my mother saw Bouchta, she'd just picked me up from school. When he greeted us with a broad smile as he opened the gate, she let out a little cry of horror: *Oi gevald, ein negger!* – Yiddish for 'How awful, a negro!' Because Bouchta, who had been born in Morocco near the Mauritanian border, in addition to being Arabic, was also black. And my mother, who had been born near the Yugoslavian border, had only seen her first black person dressed up as a cannibal at the age of fourteen at a travelling circus. Her racism was of a pre-modern sort; the subtleties of the Valladolid debate, when the Spanish conquistadors had at least considered the question of whether the Indians had a soul, would have been lost on her.

From day one, she got on with the job of getting rid of Bouchta, like the nasty black spider he was.

She began by accusing him of a thousand wrongdoings: his cooking was too heavy, which was untrue. He cleaned badly, he shrank the laundry – all also untrue. At the same time, she would say how terribly sorry she felt for him. To be the negro in this grim house next to a motorway, in the service of a madman who speaks to you like a dog and pays you a pittance, while making you bury bodies. It was awful!

For eleven years, she desperately tried to find his breaking point, to no avail. Bouchta was gentle and servile. The cupboards were full of impeccably folded linen piles smelling sweetly of lavender and the soup on the table was the perfect temperature for my father to be able eat dinner in the way he liked, that is, in four minutes flat.

And then one day, she found it.

At the age of sixty-five, Bouchta asked to take Sundays off, seeing as he was getting older and needed more rest. Carrying a plastic bag, he would head off in the morning, from the hut that had generously been fitted out for him at the bottom of the garden, and having passed through the gate of *The Estate*, instead of turning left towards the station, he would bear right towards nowhere, disappearing until seven o'clock in the evening.

'Don't you think it's odd that he turns right?' ventured my mother one evening.

'He must have found some other Arabs over that way,' replied my father, gesturing vaguely towards the yawning oblivion of the motorway.

Then one day, by chance, we spotted him overhead, on the A13 overpass, and four hours later, we saw him again in the same place but on the other side, looking in the other direction.

My mother sensed a weak point. She asked him: 'Why don't you go to Paris so you can meet other people like you instead of looking at cars go by on the overpass?'

'I don't know how to read, so I'm scared I'll get lost if I leave here,' came the honest answer.

The very next day, Bouchta had his own *Daniel et Valérie* reader and my mother began to fuss over him as if he were about to sit the entrance exam for France's top university.

'*The geese are drinking at the pond... The donkey is in the stable...*' she chanted in her heavy Jewish accent.

'*The geese are drinking at the pond... The donkey is in the stable...*' Bouchta would repeat in his Arabic accent.

He used to love those sentences, the first he had ever read and which reminded him of his farm in Tunisia. He would use them every opportunity he could, laughing, especially when he was talking to me, the sole person he used to see during the day.

Within a month, he was deciphering signs, within four he could read the newspaper. And six months later, one morning, without saying goodbye, with no warning, he was no longer there.

He left to be with other people like him, he's happy now, my mother used to say, the way you would console a child whose flea-ridden, nuisance of a pet had finally run away. How I hated her! She was speaking to me like I was some sort of imbecile about the man who had dressed me, washed me and fed me. Who had seen me grow up. To whom I had entrusted all my joys and troubles. Who had been both my father and my mother, the only person in my family endowed with any humanity. Everything pleasant I knew how to do, I owed to him, for he was kind and patient, with the patience of those who live in harmony with the trees and the seasons. As well as teaching me Moroccan and Tunisian dialect and showing me how to make gazelle horns cookies, he taught me how to care for animals and how to navigate in the dark using the stars.

Even now, when I come across a *chibani*, an old guy from the Maghreb, I can't help staring at him, searching for Bouchta in his features, even though I know it's absurd, because he'd be over a hundred by now.

The day after he left, my mother dressed up as a crime scene cleaner, in a raincoat, rubber gloves and with a mask over her mouth, and set about eradicating all trace of my darling Bouchta and the relationship between us – illegitimate in her eyes even though it was the direct result of her own apathy towards my upbringing.

She washed the walls of the room where he had slept with a mix of St Marc's household cleaning powder and bleach, and burnt all his furniture and the few meagre items he had left behind. All I had left of him was a pebble. An ordinary black pebble with a curious pattern that he had found when he was out walking. Even that she managed to steal from me and put in the bin.

Then, as if he had never spent any time with us, she simply resumed her collecting of problematic house keepers.

That evening, a little drunk, I told Philippe a light version of this story and that made me happy.

5

You'll be hungry again in an hour

While stacking my wads of cash in piles, I came across a two-hundred-euro note with writing on it, slipped in with those Scotch had given me. Normally, notes like these were in small denominations of five, and on them would be handwritten messages in all sorts of languages – things like *money is king, sovereign debt, the fallen people*, or *Politicos y banqueros, una disgracia para la nación*, or *In the name of the law, you are hereby indebted to me...* Marks left by utopians who dreamed of breaking the machine, before releasing them back into the European currency market like so many grains of sand. There was no shortage of irony in the fact that these notes would end up in the hands of drug traffickers, those paragons of capitalism.

I had never seen one worth so much. What was going on inside the head of the person who had written *you'll be hungry again in an hour* on such a big denomination, thereby risking it being declined?

Proudly I placed this very special two-hundred-euro note in the corner of *The Little Fireworks Collector's* frame like a New York hot dog vendor who frames his first dollar. It was official: the Godmother was open for business…

People were hard at work in Scotch's universe, gathering my money.

Intercept No. 8635 dated Sunday, 8 August. Intercept taken from the telephone device of the person under surveillance originating from line no. 2126456584539 the registered owner of which is not known to the Moroccan authorities. The person using the line is Karim Moufti alias Scotch. His interlocutor is Mounir Charkani alias Lizard.

Words in Arabic have been translated by Madame Patience Portefeux, who has been engaged for this purpose and who hereby jointly certifies this transcript.

Lizard: *Yo' salam aleikoum, you good or what?*
Scotch: *Hard at it, hamdoullah, the usual (laughter), except that Brandon, that fucker, now reckons he wants 60. I've told him, it's Ramadan, man, and I've asked the Godmother for a metre, see, with 70 for me and 30 for you and I dunno if she's gonna be able to do anymore… If the stupid fucker wants more, he needs to already give me money for more. Plus the price is 4.7. And I mean now, 'cos the deal's done.*
Lizard: *Yeah, yeah… you'll get the notes from me, bro'. The other dude, César, he's brought me 9.*
Scotch: *Is that it?*

Lizard: What d'you mean, is that it? Come on, man, I already got 80 and he's bringin' me the rest tomorrow, and after that I want my stuff. You better swear on the Quran you gonna bring it to me priority for 4.2.

Scotch: You's my brother, on the Quran. I know with you it's satisfied or your money back. I asked for four bags plus twenty which brings it up to a metre. And there'll be one for you plus ten, I swear on my mother's life. And if you see that fucker Brandon, you tell him I need notes to get ahead in this life.

Lizard: On the Quran of Mecca.

Scotch: If not, he can keep doin' business with his loser scrounger mate... You tell him that, on the Quran!

Lizard: Soon as I have the stuff, I'm comin' down and gettin' a good 200 end of September for two bags.

Scotch: Watch out for the size of the notes, man.

Lizard: Relax.

Scotch: Tha's cool, bro'.

Intercept No. 8642 dated Sunday, 8 August. Intercept taken from the telephone device of the person under surveillance originating from line no. 2124357981723 the registered owner of which is not known to the Moroccan authorities. The person using the line is Mounir Charkani, alias Lizard. His interlocutor is Rakir Hassani.
Words in Arabic have been translated by Madame Patience Portefeux who has been engaged for this purpose and who hereby jointly certifies this transcript.

Lizard: Hi, yeah, so...

RH: So it's not good. The guy, he told me it was good… but not right away…

Lizard: Don't talk to me about stuff that's not good. Tell me somethin' that is good. What you sayin' is there's still fuck all at your end.

RH: Yeah, yeah, still nothin'.

Lizard: Come on, cuz, even when you say you got a solution sorted, it's shit! What do you want me to tell you… I need my notes! I got no time to wait and you just takin' your time. You think it's party time, but it's not party time, bro', it's shit! I got payments to make.

RH: Anyways, I still got one more dude to see who says he got 12 for me in his hands.

Lizard: You call his mother, you call his grandmother, you call who the fuck you want, bro' but I gotta get it!

RH: It's stressin' me, too, believe me…

Lizard: Still happy, man, that you stressed… You saw the photo, bro', there be a million ass-holes lickin' my ass so I get them some of this stuff, but I'm not given' them nothin' 'cos I'm waitin' on you! So get operational, dude, and do it fast and don't come tellin' me no more that it's just a matter of time.

I had at least twenty conversations like these ones to translate each session, and from the interval between the numbers appearing in the corner of the reports, I deduced that over the past few days there had been more than two hundred of a similar type between the different protagonists involved in this deal.

Unfortunately, in their hurry to make some *fat cash*,

123

the cretins had stopped taking what they imagined were precautions in their communications, and were speaking in French, so there were fewer and fewer Arabic phrases in their conversations, meaning I was no longer able to monitor their activities.

I organised a second delivery for 15 August, this time in a spot with an even stronger stench of the guillotine than the prison parking lot: the Quai de l'Horloge, outside the Palais de Justice, directly opposite the exit from the cells. Scotch had begged me to grant him an additional week to allow him to gather the full amount; a week I had naturally refused him, bringing his deadline forward by two days for good measure, just for having dared to ask. I knew, as they did, how the capitalist game played out: the more repugnant you were, the more respect you gained.

Once again I took a taxi and again I told the driver the same story: *I've got a meeting with my nephews.* When I turned up at our meeting place, there were no longer three but five dealers waiting for me. All different versions of Scotch: bearded Islamist louts, heavy lids half concealing a breathtakingly moronic expression. One small fat one and another tall skinny one, one of whom would turn out to be – I recognised him by his voice – the famous Lizard.

The exchange went unbelievably smoothly. I succeeded in flogging four Moroccan bags in two enormous wheelie bags of forty kilos each, plus twenty kilos loose, for four hundred and fifty thousand euros in five hundred and two hundred euro notes. Scotch was a fast learner, so I demonstrated my satisfaction with him by throwing in the ten kilos I had with me in a sports bag, as a gesture of good will. There was very little talking as they were all in such a hurry to disappear from this place that was crawling with cops looking benevolently on at the adorable little Arab family exchanging bags of laundry for some poor guy on trial.

How sweet they were, those nephews of mine! When it was time to leave, I allowed myself the luxury of giving the two Moufti brothers a pinch on the cheek, doting auntie that I was – witnessed by the mobile guards – to show them just how much I loved them.

I settled my mother back into her nursing home as if she had never left, engaging the assistance of an extra pair of hands, Anta, a young woman from Madagascar, for whose devotion I could now afford to pay a fair wage. The director returned the box containing her possessions, and Schnookie the soft toy resumed his place at her bedhead. I ran into Madame Léger again in the corridor. The poor thing was no longer speaking at all, and had ended up with a hip fracture following her escapade – which didn't stop her from continuing to walk around and around in circles like an angry crustacean, pushing her aluminium frame ahead of her.

As I left *Les Eoliades,* I found her two children sitting on a bench, in mid argument. The Léger daughter was weeping hot tears, while her brother shouted over her as he gnawed at the skin around his nails, his face undone with anxiety. An infinite sadness emanated from the two of them, both in their fifties, who had now been carrying their pain for nine months, like one of those heavy, two-handled baskets you lug around the grocery store. Their father had recently been moved to my floor and no matter what time I went past his room, he would always be leaning forward, strapped into his armchair, and weeping.

'They tell us that old people need to keep themselves hydrated, but I'm always finding the little Evian bottles I bring in because nobody gives him anything to drink, and they're sitting there unopened... And the days I'm not there to feed him, they just put the meal-tray down in his room and close the door. *Bon appétit, Monsieur Léger*, they say, but nobody gives a damn whether he actually eats or not... And did you see how they've dressed Mother? It's 35 degrees and she's wearing a woollen jumper... And her escape... That car just knocked her down on the slip road like a dog... Can you imagine if she had got any further? And how dare they ask us to pay for that anti-wandering bracelet she ripped off! I'd like to know where all our money goes.'

Each new grievance would set off the daughter's sobs again. The situation of that family was so ghastly she could have gone on for hours, and it was a story I knew off by heart.

'It's always like that over summer, with staff away on holidays. If you like, you can share the extra carer I've taken on for my mother...'

'Oh yes, that would be fantastic...' she said to me, eyes full of gratitude.

Her brother intervened immediately, to explain that

unfortunately they had no way of paying for it. Their two families would be staying in Paris that summer and they would take it in turns at their parents' bedside.

'We're completely skint. My father's pension barely covers half his expenses, and as for my mother, it's all coming out of our pockets. We spend our time counting our money. We asked them about applying for guardianship, but everybody tells us it's a white elephant… over-complicated and not worth the effort. First you have to wait a year to get it before a judge and once the decision is made, the accounts are blocked and you can't withdraw another cent for months except with a judge's authorisation which you never get either because the judge is over-worked or he's away on holiday.'

'So what are you meant to do? Fake your parents' signature to withdraw their pension money from their accounts?'

'Precisely.'

'You know, we're all in the same boat…'

'We need at least ten thousand euros a month to cover all the costs. It's huge. The notary advised us to sell their apartment for a life annuity and then bank the income in our accounts. We've been advertising for six months now, but nobody's interested in such an expensive annuity transaction. It won't be long before I have to sell my own apartment to pay for this damned nursing home.'

'Where's your parents' apartment?'

'On Rue Monge. A three-room place with 72 square metres.'

'Actually, you know, I might be interested! I'll be

straight with you: as long as the initial capital payment is very small, I'm prepared to pay you what you need as a monthly annuity.'

Hope was dawning in their eyes.

'You could take on an extra full-time aide for the two of them and then take it in turns between you so one of you, at least, can have a holiday... But your parents will have to sign the contract in front of a notary, and all that...'

'Our notary is willing to go into nursing homes and get old people to sign things – no matter what condition they're in – provided there's no chance of anyone suing. We're the only two children and you only have to look at our parents to see they're never coming out of here.'

'As I said, I'm interested.'

'You do realise you'd be saving our lives?'

'There is just one small thing. I can pay you whatever annuity you want, but it has to be in cash. I'm not going to lie to you, I have a large amount at home that belongs to my mother. It's not dirty money, just the savings of an old and slightly mad Jewish woman who always thought it was just a matter of time before the Germans came after her again.'

'We can deposit the money into our account, that's not a problem,' said the Léger daughter.

'No, no, we can't do that!' objected the son.

'Well then, we're never going to manage!' she said, with a display of dramatic despair, as if the fact that you weren't supposed to launder money was her brother's fault. She began to sob again, and he resumed his sighing.

'If it makes you feel any better, the director of *Les Eoliades* is not at all particular. On the contrary, I'd say the cash would allow her to pay for thousands of hours overtime off the books. Perhaps you don't realise, but this place is owned by an American pension fund that greatly appreciates any money it can save on its staff.'

'OK, I'll raise it with the notary. It's true, when you're in our situation, you can't afford too delicate a conscience.'

'What do you do for work, if you don't mind my asking?'

'I'm a detective.'

'Small world! My partner is too – and I'm a court translator.'

There we all were, part of that great, middle-class mass being strangled by its elderly. It was reassuring.

The Léger children would have sold their parents' apartment for around 750,000 euros, so we agreed on a capital sum of 50,000 and an annuity of 20,000 a month for the life of their hemiplegic and aphasic 86-year-old father and their mother with Alzheimer's – a period of time estimated generously at three years, given the desperate look of them. So, nobody was being conned. As the papers for the apartment had already been drawn up in preparation for a possible sale, and obtaining a loan is a formality when you already own a mortgageable property, it took barely a week for my bank to lend me the money for the capital sum and the purchase of my life annuity.

*

Meanwhile, I went to visit my future property with the
Léger son.

Whether because he felt awkward about entering the
private realm of his parents, or else from some basic, ani-
malistic psychological reaction in the face of death, he
declined to cross the threshold, but encouraged me with
a wave to make myself at home. Inside, it smelt musty.
Dust particles danced in a ray of sunlight which filtered
through the drawn curtains, revealing a dirty interior
in very poor upkeep – but nothing, I estimated, that
would defeat a Polish handyman. The cupboards, which
I opened one by one, were filled with clothes and old bits
and pieces covered in a patina of grime. It would all have
to be thrown out, and I knew that once again I would
be the one burdened with that task. It even entered my
mind that the Légers were happy to offload their parents'
place just so they didn't have to sort through their things.

First my father, then my husband, my mother and
now other people's parents: you had to wonder if I wasn't
somehow destined to clear people's lives of their worldly
possessions, one rubbish bag at a time. Regardless, the
apartment was in a great location, only a few metres from
the remains of the Arènes de Lutèce. I was delighted – at
last I had something decent to pass on to my girls.

As we all sat around the notary's large desk, I buried my
hands into the side pockets of my summer dress and
rolled my two fat wads of twenty thousand euros around
between my fingers and the palm of my hand. Like two
fat pebbles. When the time came and everything had

been signed, I laid my pebbles on the table. Luc Léger grabbed them, the way you might pick up something a little dodgy, swiftly offloading them into the hands of his sister and scrawling me a receipt for two months' rent. He may have found it all distasteful, but it was clear from the sparkle in her eyes that she was fond of a bit of dough.

Summer flashed by at top speed, and then it was the start of autumn… Attacks, strikes, heatwaves…

My daughters returned from their holidays and went back to work. Philippe took three weeks' holiday with his son to show him some African giraffes; and I busied myself with my new apartment which I cleared out and had completely renovated for 60,000 euros by one Mikolaj and his team.

I also took myself off for a few days to Switzerland, where, incidentally, they had just adopted a law against money laundering and had placed a ceiling on cash payments of… 90,000 euros per transaction. I went down to the Hotel Belvedere – the one in the photo of *The Little Fireworks Collector* – where, in days gone by, I had known my way around; I was determined to enjoy myself and to start my *endless summer* at last.

It was my grandmother, Rosa, who had started the trend for holidaying in this mythical hotel in 1946, with the money she had inherited from her new husband. Her sister Ilona, who had sought refuge in London at the time of the Anschluss, had established a philanthropic foundation over there, whose members were very, very old gentlemen, barely aware they were alive, but who were prepared to come to the aid of good, deported Jewish women. And so it was that my grandmother had married a certain 92-year-old Mr Williams in his home in November 1945, a man she had known for five minutes, all the time it took to strip every one of his heirs of their inheritance. He was dead within a few months of the ceremony and after having *come into money* – after all, one could hardly sue a good Jewish deportee – she paid for herself and her daughter, my mother, to do what together they had dreamed of in the camp: take a long and luxurious holiday in a neutral, German-speaking country, eating cakes while looking out at a lake. And that's how the very chic English lady by the name of *Mrs Rose Williams* paved the way for future generations of her family at the Belvedere – in the process kicking off her own *endless summer*, which unfortunately only lasted fifteen years or so because her body, worn out by the deprivations it had suffered during the war, gave out at the age of about sixty.

I'm under no illusions – had it instead been *Rosa Zielberman*, the pleb from the Prater district, who had attempted to make the reservation for that month of August in 1946, she would have received the pleasant reply that the hotel was fully booked, and none of us would ever have set foot in the place.

My father came to join the two women in 1955 and I joined them in 1963, after my birth. It became a family custom to start our summer travels with a stay at the Belvedere so my mother could recover from her exhausting year of doing nothing. We used to book from one year to the next and would always arrive on the same dates so we could enjoy the fireworks on the 1st of August. My husband replaced my father at our side and my daughters were born. Then he died, leaving behind an all female table setting, until my mother was no longer able to pay for our holiday. After a long absence, here I was returning alone for the first time.

Known around the world for its magnificent view over the lake, the Belvedere had been in the same family since its establishment in the 19th century. Three generations of Hürschs had greeted my relatives in their solid building with the scowling expressions of the professional Swiss hotelier. Their ultra-Calvinist austerity effectively kept away all the *nouveaux riches* and the wops, who would find in the hotel none of the noisy distractions which they craved. No spa, no swimming pool, no hotel boutique, no conference room. No background music of the synthesised whale song variety, no video game room with screaming kids running around. Nothing but silence and an unobstructed view, in return for an astronomical bill. That was true luxury, the sort that created a sense of exclusivity. The last time I had set foot there, back when my mother still had a bit of money, I'd heard somebody ask at reception whether there was Internet. Monsieur Hürsch had replied contemptuously that he *did not offer that sort of service*, as if they'd been asking for prostitutes.

But when my taxi dropped me at the entrance, I didn't recognise a thing. The hotel had disappeared, or rather it had been swallowed up by a glass mega-structure in the shape of a parallelepiped. Not a single familiar face remained amongst either the clientele or the staff, as if the Hürschs had never existed. No more little chocolate on my goose down duvet. In fact, no more feathered duvet at all in my aseptic, taupe-coloured room. Everything had become beige and taupe – curtains, bedspread, carpet… The non-colours *par excellence*, that you marry with white and black to create the 'cocooning chic' look of every luxury hotel in the world.

The view over the lake was still there, of course, except that if you lowered your eyes, a hideous extension had replaced the pretty gardens where the *little fireworks collector* had taken her first steps. It was when I saw niqabs circling in the Swiss-blue sky under the petal-shaped wings of para-gliders that the penny finally dropped: the Belvedere had been swallowed up by a sovereign wealth fund from the Gulf.

As my gaze followed those little black bells, I let out a sigh of philosophical weariness. Among all the veiled little girls sitting on the terrace of the Belvedere, their noses tilted skywards, was there perhaps one who might be allowed a strawberry melba ice cream drowning in sugar syrup and Chantilly cream? And if such a girl existed, was she too busy dreaming, as I had at her age, of living a life less ordinary?

I deposited my things in my mole-coloured hole so I could go and wander the shopping streets without further ado and buy everything I had always coveted, and which I could finally afford. But I realised very quickly, walking past the jewellers' and fashion boutiques, that I didn't feel like any of it. I had barely paused in front of the platinum, gold or caviar-infused anti-aging cream at 600 euros for 300mls, when the sales girl, like a lab assistant in her white coat, appeared: *It's not just a simple anti-aging cream, Madame, it's an experience.* Smearing rare metals or animals on the road to extinction onto my face in order to achieve eternal youth bordered on the stuff of metaphysics... *You might as well just eat the money – chop it up and make a luxury nutritional supplement, like royal jelly*, I thought, making only myself laugh.

In the end, I contented myself with being a so-called '*Japanese ant*': that is, with laundering my money by buying four Fancy Vivid Pink 0.5 carat diamonds at 90,000 euros each (to be stored in a lip-stick), as well as a Hermès Kelly bag in red crocodile for the same price, all of which would be resold at auction on my return to Paris. Pink diamonds and brand-name handbags sell like hotcakes, something I knew from my ogling of Parisian auction house sales catalogues. The only personal item I permitted myself was a terribly expensive Italian leather collar for DNA and a matching leash.

After this spot of shopping, I returned to my hotel, alone and silent, and spent my first evening on my balcony, admiring my elegant dog, lost in thought.

My *endless summer* had not begun at all how I had imagined it.

I was supposed to be overjoyed to be *blowing some dough, some moolah,* to borrow the language of the intellectuals currently populating my life... Yes... but buy what, do what? I was certain that not a single one of the young dealers whose conversations I had been translating for almost twenty-five years had had to cope with looking after a vomiting child, or one with braces, or with paying for school trips, or threading cords back through hoodies – or any of the small realities that threaten to drown women in the quicksand of motherhood. Life had run over me, like the iron I had used every evening so my children, despite the shortage of money, always wore impeccable clothes. I had become a bourgeois *petite madame,* my wings clipped by material preoccupations. And, contrary to what the ads would have us believe, it was not at all clear how you were supposed to alter your behaviour, once all those habits had become ingrained.

I ordered my dinner from room service. It goes without saying that there was no Saint-Gallen sausage on the menu, but instead an oxymoron by the name of *Luxury Halal Cuisine.*

I went to bed early. As soon as I fell asleep, the sewage system that served as my unconscious overflowed, flooding my mind with a continuous stream of incoherent scraps of dreams: me waiting for Scotch, my feet sinking into burning hot summer asphalt; Philippe fastening my Magnum around his nude torso like it was his service weapon; DNA swallowing mouthfuls of water, desperately trying to cool down his sausage-shaped body in the freezing water of the lake, tail wagging furiously… In the end, I got up at five in the morning with a head full of metal filings and a desperate need to talk to somebody. I called Philippe, and then, ashamed, changed my mind. He called me straight back but I didn't answer. Out in the hotel garden, it was already all go, thanks to the *Al Fajr* – the favourite prayer of the Prophet, who must have been a morning person. I headed down towards the lake for an invigorating dip, but that wasn't to be either; a family of extremely threatening swans blocked my path.

At six o'clock, I was at breakfast, pensively buttering my *Weggli*. These typically Swiss bread rolls bear a striking resemblance to a pair of buttocks, a fact that suddenly struck me as scandalously *haram*. What the hell were the Qatari management up to? For the second time since arriving at the Belvedere, I found myself laughing alone. The rest of my day stretched before me like the road to Calvary.

By midday, I was on the train home.

The first thing that leaped out at me when I opened the door to my apartment was my banana-coloured two hundred euro banknote stuck into the frame of *The Little Fireworks Collector*.

All of a sudden, the meaning of the message written on it seemed both crystal clear and troublingly apt. *You'll be hungry again in an hour* is what you say to children when they feed themselves rubbish – and it was precisely the conclusion I had reached during my lightning trip to Switzerland. What I needed wasn't piles of cash to splash; nor was I interested in climbing the social ladder. No… I just wanted to rediscover a bit of the little fireworks collector's innocence. I realised there wouldn't be any *endless summer* as long as I was unable to rid myself of my anxiety about what tomorrow would bring, the anxiety I had lived with for so many years. Before I could spend a cent on myself, I had to accumulate sufficient money so that my girls would each at least have a roof over their head.

Until that point had been reached, I would count my pennies like a shopkeeper. *Then we'll see if I'm hungry*, I said to myself.

6

Talk doesn't cook rice

Like any good shopkeeper, every time I opened the door to my basement, I despaired at seeing my stock levels fall so slowly.

Colette Fò, my neighbour from across the landing, must have been thinking more or less the same thing herself, because she looked as preoccupied as I did whenever we crossed paths in the lift, each with our big bags. I decided to break the ice and dive straight in, getting right to the point:

'Tell me, Madame Fò, would it bother you if I were to pay my building and administration fees in cash this quarter?'

The first decision the Fòs had made once they had majority ownership in the building was to sack the property manager and take over management of the whole building themselves.

I had never noticed to what extent this morose creature was a Chinese version of myself. Similarly dressed in grey or black off-the-rack outfits, always carrying a plastic bag, up at 6 am and never in bed before midnight, and with the whole family apparently relying on her with no support from any *Monsieur Fò*, whom I imagined to be dead or somewhere in prison. You only had to look at her to see that she too was getting no pleasure from the capital she was accumulating; and it was substantial capital, seeing as she owned at least four bars-tabacs in the neighbourhood and I don't know how many apartments.

Her gaze settled on me, and I could feel her weighing me up as if to assess my future usefulness in the shorter or longer term.

'You have too much cash?'

'You could say that.'

'Me, buy your apartment for market value plus cash less 30% commission.'

'The apartment's worth 540. So if I give you 300 in cash, you buy it from me for 750 and you keep 90, right? 90's a lot, isn't it? Laundering is usually 20%.'

We also had that in common: I was quick with numbers.

'Lots of work to make money disappear.'

'I'll think about it. 90,000 euros commission is quite a bit.'

And we each went home. With my Hermès bag and my pink diamonds, I had potentially laundered 500,000 euros. The sale of my apartment would add another 200,000 to that; then there was my life annuity which was a work in progress. It was all beginning to take shape.

Towards the end of November, I was given a new series of translations in a case involving far greater quantities of drugs than the amounts I was dealing with my bunch of losers. It involved Tunisians, some of whom were based in the West Indies and who were importing cocaine from Colombia – which they were paying for in hash. In tonnes of hash. But I didn't dare make contact with them as I had with Scotch because the file originated with the Central Bureau for Drug Control and I was suspicious that the guys I was listening to had been recruited by the police to set up 'fake genuine' deliveries.

That's how things were done these days at the Central Bureau. It was the modern way: *no clean policing without dirty policing*. It meant you could schedule the drug seizures for the TV cameras, and have the ministers pose, looking suitably po-faced, in front of mountains of hash.

All I knew was that this sort of dodgy business allowed some traffickers to live like Saudi princes with the State's blessing, which absolutely removed any scruples – just in case one day I should acquire some – about doing the same thing myself. But really, what a disgrace, if you stop to think about it, these cops who are paid by the taxpayer, wallowing in the lap of luxury along with the dealers.

With my current business partner, at least I could be completely confident. Sure, he dined at the local kebab joint. But it wouldn't have occurred to anybody to recruit him for anything. Nonetheless, I kept those Tunisians in the back of my mind. Actually, I was jealous because I would have liked to do it like the cops: work with intelligent people under good conditions. Unlike the clowns with whom I was forced to do business, those guys had taste, hung out at five-star hotels, treated their girlfriends or wives with respect – women who weren't poor illiterate girls brought up from the *bled*. Unlike the more half-witted type of Muslim, they did not hold the view that you could *never leave the belly of a woman without child, nor her back without a rod*. And that was precisely what I found so damned fishy as I listened to the Tunisians through my headphones. Because Scotch, to take just one example – and they were all alike, these dealers, with rare exceptions – was already looking for a mate, despite having barely started to attain a degree of prosperity. To this end, he had been in touch with his Moroccan family so they could find him, and I quote, *a good woman who wears the niqab and reads the Quran*.

Still, I had the partners I was able to afford, the only ones stupid enough to do business with a woman who had materialised out of nowhere. Besides, they had all worked hard over the summer and were now making contact again by SMS with a view to relieving me of a further two hundred kilos on 15 October.

1 m = 2 x 40 + 20, no +, at 3.5 in 2 x

Unfortunately, even though I always ordered a taxi with a big boot, you couldn't ever fit more than two forty-kilo wheeled bags, plus one more with twenty kilos of loose gear.

Where to with the Tati bags? Scotch asked, paving the way for some humorous banter.

I shot back my reply: *Tati store – wedding dresses, next to the change rooms, 5.15pm.*

I was in a good mood.

On the morning of the day of the delivery, I was called in urgently by the Robbery and Serious Crime Squad to draw up an inventory of the contents of a box, as well as a hard drive containing items written in Arabic which had been seized during a search the night before at the home of two thieves who had just been arrested. Two young guys specialising in geriatric home invasions, and whose *modus operandi* consisted of passing themselves off as gas company employees.

I sat down in one of the offices and emptied the box, item after item, noting down, as I'd been asked to do, everything I found – namely, the perfect internet-Islamist kit.

1) One text in Arabic entitled *The Solution*: speech given by Tamin Al Adnani, a jihadist who died in 1989 after fighting against the USSR in Afghanistan.

2) One text in Arabic: *The Obligations of Jihad* by Abdallah Azzam, known as *the heart and brain of the Afghan jihad*, who died in Peshawar in 1989.

3) One booklet: *The Meeting*, sub-titled *Rules to follow when recruiting an aspiring new jihadist*. Author unknown.

4) One booklet: *The Lawfulness of Martyrdom Operations*. Author unknown.

5) One CD with a sleeve containing an Arabic text entitled *Democratia* that included a 120 minute long speech by Sheik Abu Musab al Zarkawi.

The audio version of the speech was interrupted by sounds of gunshots and jihadist singing…

And that's why I refused to do translations in terrorism cases. It wasn't the first time I had done this sort of work and you always found the same sort of intellectual hardware with these types who had been radicalised via the internet. People think that the translator helps to foil plots… Well, maybe one time in every thousand they provide some assistance in this regard, but the 999 other translations they do involve hours of exegesis of the words of the Prophet (may the peace and blessings of Allah be upon him) written by moronic cretins, radicalised by reading the *Quran for idiots*. It's unbearable!

6) A 16-minute video showing jihadists slitting soldiers' throats.
7) A collection of war-like hadiths entitled *Paradise is our Reward*.
8) Two photos: Mahdi Al-Yahawi and Jaber Al-Khashnawi, *inghimasi* from Le Bardo in Tunisia bathing in a sea of blood.
9) A video of Abu Mohammed Al-Adnani entitled *To the Soldiers of the Caliphate of Europe*…

While I was conscientiously making a note of all this to an audio backdrop of chanted poems, a young cop from the unit came over. He was a sweet, sporty kid I'd been working with for a couple of years, who believed in the triumph of good over evil and who always smelt of mint chewing gum. In response to his querying look, I showed him the photo of Al Baghdadi on the CD I was playing; for the occasion, he had abandoned his troglodyte al-Qaeda look in favour of something more modern, having trimmed his beard and put on some black clothes.

'They're *nasheeds*, a capella versions...'

'Do you mind turning them off? They're freaking me out...'

'It's nothing weird... they're ancient Islamic poems, the purpose of which is to direct people in their daily decisions... And they're full of truths.'

'Sounds like the stuff they put on Daesh propaganda videos.'

He picked up my list and, having glanced over it, put it back down with a big sigh. It was a typical 21st-century sigh. My daughters let out the same sort of sigh when they see the corpses of children washed up on beaches, forests burning, animals dying...

'It's the *Salil Al-Sawarim*... If you want to know, there's also a very risqué belly-dance version... There's even one by the Chipmunks. It's just a very ancient song with the same lyrics as *La Marseillaise* more or less... only not as hard-core!' I said, trying to get a smile out of him, but to no avail.

I continued: 'You know, these so-called *inventories*... they always throw up some pretty freaky results.'

'But when is all this going to stop?'

'What are you talking about? Don't you think there are worse things to worry about in the world than a handful of losers with diseased brains looking for their fifteen minutes of glory? Get over it already – all they've done is invent a new way of dying that's as random as cancer or car accidents.'

Conversations with me become disheartening very, very quickly.

'… listen, I came to find you because we need a hand. None of these dickheads want to speak in French and they're making out they don't understand a word. Just five minutes, as long as it takes to translate their rights, and then we're sending them over to counter intelligence.'

'OK. Five minutes. But you're going to pay me the whole hour, and that's on top of my time for the inventory.'

'Fine.'

So I went to take a seat next to one of the two Islamist-geriatric-robbers. And while I was certifying the statement in my capacity as translator, this guy, taking advantage of a moment's distraction on the part of the armed officer standing next to him, grabbed his service revolver and took a shot at the cop, missed him, and then shot himself in the head, splattering me with his brains.

It happened in the blink of an eye.

A moment's silence followed that seemed like an age, as if time had stopped, then suddenly all hell broke loose with hysterical screaming and crying followed by a parade of cops who appeared from every floor. To complete the scene, a swarm of psych counsellors dispatched by police headquarters descended on the Serious Crime Squad offices like grasshoppers.

As for me, I was sitting on a chair in the corner of the

room, with little pieces of bloodied grey matter stuck to the shoulder of my brand new crêpe blouse, bought in anticipation of a meal out with Philippe whom I hadn't seen since his return from Africa… And as nobody offered me so much as a glass of water, in the end I went home.

In a zombie-like state, I pulled on the Godmother's work outfit of raincoat, sunglasses and hijab – and then proceeded to make a whole series of careless moves, the first of which was to bring DNA along because I hadn't had time to take him out.

I loaded my one hundred kilos of hash into the boot of my car, and drove three streets away to park. From there I tried to call a taxi, but as none were available, I hailed one down randomly in the street. Between the ones who didn't want to take an animal and the ones who thought my load was too bulky, I had to wait thirty minutes for a Chinese guy who picked me up along with my enormous bags and my dog and headed for the Tati store. As I was running late, I failed to case the place – a serious lapse of prudence. At 5.05pm, my driver pulled up on Boulevard de Rochechouart on the far side of the Metro tracks which run above ground there. On the way I'd tried to call Philippe to cancel our plans for the evening after what had happened at work, but it went through to voicemail; so I left him a message. I asked the taxi to wait for me with my dog, offering to pay extra because he was bellyaching. I hurried across the area beneath the tracks and crossed the Boulevard to the Tati store located on the other side, looking for my nephews.

At 5.12pm, as I was making my way at full speed to the wedding dress department, I was almost knocked over by Philippe and two of his men as they rushed past.

They hadn't spotted me. I turned tail immediately and headed back to my taxi, calling Scotch on the way.

'Where are you?'

'We're late. We're jammed on Boulevard de Rochechouart.'

'The place is crawling with police. I'll wait for you further up the Boulevard, at the square. Leave your mates and run up here on foot with the money. They can go around the traffic island in the car and come past on the other side to pick up the merchandise.'

Back in the taxi, the Chinese driver gave me grief about the hairs DNA had supposedly shed all over his back seat. It wasn't the moment to pick a fight, so I took the dog out and brought him with me, thereby making myself instantly identifiable on any and every surveillance camera. I headed up the street towards the square, and saw Scotch approaching in a hurry. He had some sort of big monogrammed bag slung across his body, bouncing around on his stomach. which ought to have contained my money. I say *ought* because I was convinced it was empty, otherwise DNA, who was trained in both drugs and currency detection, would have picked him out, like he did at my place when he was surrounded by large wads of notes.

I couldn't prove it, but I was absolutely certain that bag did not contain my 350,000 euros.

'You brought the cops with you,' I said.

'I didn't bring anything. Come on, let's get going.'

'We're not going anywhere!'

I stared at him, not moving.

Scotch, very close to hitting me, clenched his fists. Instantly, DNA bared his teeth and began to growl in an extremely impressive manner.

At last the car made it to the top of the Boulevard.

'I think we'll just leave it there, shall we?'

Scotch hesitated, furious, then went back to join his four mates and together they took off back down Boulevard de Rochechouart, passing my taxi on the way, and not making the connection, thank God, that it was the vehicle which had brought me there along with the drugs.

A few minutes later I left, retracing my route back to my basement with my one hundred kilos.

I hadn't managed to cancel Philippe's visit. It played out in a fog. He turned up at my place at around 8pm, just after I had got back in, carrying some kind of small rose bush to celebrate our reunion. It was only when DNA started sniffing the traces of brain left on my crêpe blouse that I realised I had not yet changed.

'Shit, my blouse is fucked.'

My head was a complete blank and my ears were buzzing. I looked at Philippe with his dwarf rose bush. In order to *take me out*, he was wearing a shirt and tie of the kind you might find in a basket of reduced items at the sales, and I could picture the beetle-wing shaped sweat stains on his back. All of a sudden, he looked exactly like what he was: a cop.

'Do you want to talk about it?'

'About what?'

I looked at him.

'About your day...'

'No, why?'

Philippe nodded solemnly. A rational person trying to make sense of the irrational behaviour of the person he was talking to: *the poor woman, she's in shock, she's refusing to verbalise her trauma*, he was saying to himself. But I was simply dealing with the morning's events in my customary way, by adding said event to its place in my mental list of horrors.

'I'm really sorry not to have picked up when you called me, but I was in the middle of running an operation.'

Faced with my silence and the wild look I had about me, he bravely racked his brains for something to say – and ended up telling me about his failed ambush. When he'd arrived at the Tati store, there'd been three guys, three Moroccans – God knows where they'd come from – who were clearly also waiting for Scotch and the Godmother as they fiddled with the dresses.

'Can you imagine? Six dudes in the wedding dress department, three Arab crims and three cops, while a group of chicks are oohing and aahing at their girlfriend coming out of the changing room who's dressed like a meringue. It was surreal. We took a look around, sized things up. It was obvious the set-up was blown, so we checked their I.D. Three Moroccans from the *bled*, passports in order, all supposedly there to choose a wedding dress...! They must have been waiting for that loser Karim Moufti who's somehow – and who the fuck knows how – dealing top-grade Moroccan gear, that every Paris A-lister is fighting over... And for the Godmother, no doubt, who's imported it I don't know how or stolen it from I don't know where. I looked at the store's CCTV on the ground floor, but there are so many potential godmothers it's impossible to know if she turned up or not. I'm sick to death of this whole business. I've asked the judge for a warrant to track the Cayenne and we're staking out his place. Next time, we're arresting everybody.'

Up to that point, on the rare occasions Philippe had referred to the Godmother, I'd always had the feeling he was talking about somebody else. I realise this reaction fits perfectly with the clinical profile of a psychopath: a lying machine, efficient, devoid of emotion, capable of acting in a state of complete moral compartmentalisation. But that evening it was different: the more he told me about his bungled arrest, the larger the space he seemed to be occupying in my apartment – like something that might turn hostile as it grew and grew. He must have sensed it because, with a worried look, he took my face between his hands to kiss me. I tried to force myself to return his kiss, but my body felt so heavy I could barely move.

He stroked the back of my neck then took me vigorously into his arms.

'I've missed you, I've missed your body... One month... we haven't seen each other in over a month...'

He tried to take off my blouse and I just let him do it, limp as a rag doll. His face was flushed and I could have sworn he was panting. Then, all of a sudden, confronted by my inertia, he had second thoughts.

'Listen, I shouldn't… It's not a good time… You should rest after what you've been through.' He put me to bed and I fell asleep instantly.

I woke up at around two in the morning to find a yellow dwarf rosebush on my bedside table. I tried to go back to sleep but with that plant there, I couldn't. In the end, I had to get up and throw it down the rubbish chute on the landing.

So I had a lot on my mind as October came around.

At *Les Eoliades*, at least, a dead calm reigned, as my mother tyrannised the poor Anta whom I was paying a small fortune to endure on a daily basis the suffering I had offloaded onto her. Outside, it was autumn, and it rained every day like it does on those inhospitable planets in sci-fi movies, while on the TV, special news items taught people how to tie a tourniquet in the event of a limb being blown off by a bomb. As for my drug-dealing business, I was making Scotch sweat it out until he confessed and apologised for having tried to rip me off.

I called him every morning on WhatsApp. I was done with the phone, because while I could carefully change the odd word here and there in my translations, I had torn my hair out trying to falsify the conversation outside the Tati store so it would pass unnoticed and whoever was reading the transcripts would think the Godmother had never showed up.

Each time he would pick up and scream at me in some bastard hybrid of French and Arabic that because of me, his customers were making his life a living hell. But as he refused to confess and apologise, I simply hung up on him.

He held out a week!

'So, I'm on Avenue Henri Barbusse and there are cops in a green Renault parked outside your place, and you can't go anywhere without others tailing you…'

'How do you know where I live?'

'Your dumb-ass questions are boring the shit out of me… I've left a plan, in French, in your letterbox, which I want you to follow to the letter. I'm warning you – if you stray from the program in the slightest way, even the tiniest detail, I'm done with this for good. You understand what I'm saying?'

I was speaking to him in Arabic and, even though I articulated every word as though he were mentally disabled, I was never quite sure if he understood everything I said.

'Yes, madame.'

'Repeat it back.'

'I read the piece of paper and I do exactly what's written down on the paper otherwise it's finished…'

'It's finished forever. Repeat it back to me…'

'Forever.'

'That's right.'

Now that the group was being tailed, the big deliveries we had been doing were out of the question. To avoid having to change vehicle and play cat-and-mouse, I came up with the idea of incorporating the transactions into the dealers' everyday routines so that the police, even if they were following them, wouldn't suspect a thing.

The Godmother's plan revolved around two axes: we're going to help mum with her shopping and we're going to lose some weight at the swimming pool.

When the Moufti family was planning to go to the supermarket – which was always around 6pm (when it was busiest) – Scotch would call the Godmother's phone an hour beforehand, so she could set things in motion. If she couldn't, she would send a WhatsApp message saying 'no'.

If the deal was on, she would head to the supermarkets at Drancy, Bondy or Romainville (all places with no shortage of veiled women) and deposit a blue bag containing ten kilos of hash concealed beneath some vegetables at the left luggage service, in exchange for a numbered tag. She would then push her trolley around, while Scotch or his brother took a packet of Chamonix Orange cakes from the shelf, leaving an envelope with 40,000 euros under the packet below (I was now selling the hash for 4,000 to punish him. *Listen, Monsieur Moufti, the minute I do it for 3.5 a kilo you rip me off, I got the message; you think the price is too cheap...*) along with a second tag for a bag, also blue, also containing vegetables.

Why Chamonix Oranges? Because nobody born after 1980 still eats those sickly sweet things with their improbable shape – and because the base of the packet is the size of a C5 envelope.

Anyway, the Godmother would then collect the

envelope containing her money as well as the tag for the other blue bag, at the same time as she, too, took a packet of cakes (I adore Chamonix Orange cakes), replacing the tag with her own (after surreptitiously checking the money). She would then happily continue with her shopping, pay at the cash register, before going to collect the second blue bag, while one of the two Moufti boys would return to the Chamonix Oranges to pick up a second packet along with the new bag storage tag and any other item from the same shelf (I insisted on this point to remove suspicion from what might otherwise have appeared to be a routine on the CCTV). Then, after paying at the till for the packets of cakes as well as for mum's shopping, he would pick up the original blue bag containing the hash.

At around the same time, the Moufti family started swimming twice a week at the Georges-Hermant pool in the 19th arrondissement.

In locker 120, code 2402 (a locker which was always empty because it was the one furthest away from where you had to tap in your code), a sports bag, this time with fifteen kilos, would be awaiting its future owner in exchange for an envelope and another sports bag, identical but empty. There were no cameras in the changing rooms, so the Godmother could swim in complete anonymity with her cap and goggles on, crossing paths in the lanes with two fat, ungainly, frozen seals, namely Scotch and his brother. It was winter, and it was cold as hell. I like cold water – those two, not so much. It was pretty funny.

The results… At the supermarket – October: 3 deliveries; November: 7; December: 7; January: 4. At the pool – October: 2; November: 8; December: 8; January: 4.

After two deliveries where everything went smoothly, I lowered my prices back to 3,500 a kilo.

I'd shifted a total of 540 kilos, but the work! And I was only packing and delivering, whereas they were cutting, weighing, re-packaging, selling, collecting the cash, finding buyers, converting into bigger denominations, laundering… They looked like death warmed up and, as it happens, were losing quite a bit of weight. When magistrates treat dealers as layabouts, they truly show how little they understand about the vast amount of work involved in the drug industry.

I knew that Philippe must be tearing his hair out. The few telephone intercepts I had been given to translate evoked a banal, small-time drugs operation with only fifty kilos finding its way to market every week. The reason he hadn't decided to bring in Scotch and his little friends (who, it seemed, were growing in numbers, given the personnel needed for this sort of dealing) was because he was still running after the Godmother, and it was sending him crazy. Despite his relentless analysis of the transcripts, and even going so far as to view on loop the CCTV footage of the gangs' most frequented hangouts, he was drawing a blank.

And then half way through January, a series of strange things happened.

On the 10th, after one of my swimming pool transactions – I remember the date because Scotch's whole gang ended up getting arrested soon afterwards, on the 20th), I'd arranged to meet the Léger daughter outside the BHV store to pay my monthly annuity. We had a coffee together, ranted about the director of the nursing home, and I took 20,000 euros out of the envelope to give her. Then, with the remaining 32,500, I went into the store where I had a manicure appointment, my first in 25 years.

I was going to town: would my nails be baby pink, navy blue or lime green? I had been happily tormented by this issue for a week.

I don't know if it was the smell of the varnish or because I was tired after my swim but I passed out and fell off the chair in the Nail Bar, gashing my head.

The paramedics gathered me up, with my bloodied face, and took me off to hospital, and as they rummaged around in my handbag looking for some identification, they immediately came across the envelope. When I regained consciousness, they asked me if a relative could be notified, as I was suffering heart failure and they had to keep me in so I could be seen by a cardiologist.

As soon as I heard the words *notify a relative*, I tore off all the things stuck to my chest like a woman possessed, and jumped out of bed in my underwear in a total state of panic.

'I'm completely fine… Now give me back my things!'

'We can't let you leave.'

'Yes you can, you just have to inform me of the consequences of my decision to leave – so, there, I'm informed. I'm perfectly informed. Now give me the papers to sign and hand me back my things.'

The intern gave me a super suspicious look as he held out my bag with one hand, and my envelope with the other.

'Yes – you found an envelope containing 32,500 euros in cash… Big deal! I'm sure you'd love an explanation, but frankly, I don't have to give you any… So – hand it over!' And I snatched the envelope from his hands.

I left the hospital in as dignified a fashion as I could manage, and took a taxi home.

So my heart is giving out too, I thought, on arriving back home. And because I really did have other fish to fry, I took the information for what it was, namely something that would have to be dealt with in future, nothing more.

For as long as I can remember, my father had had to take his *drops for his heart*. From time to time, I would see him sit down on a bench, out of breath. One drop, two drops… and hop, he would be off again like a Duracell bunny whose batteries had just been changed. When he was about sixty, a pacemaker was suggested because the notorious drops were no longer up to the job. He refused.

It was over a platter of shellfish at La Coupole on Boulevard du Montparnasse, while greedily slurping down oysters, that he announced to us his decision to retire from life, much the way he would have told us he was going to retire from business. He had already started to dissolve Mondiale and to divide up its assets between all of his employees. At the same time, he'd accumulated in his safe deposit box a large stash of Krugerrands, those pretty South African gold coins each weighing an ounce and minted with the image of a springbok. Worth more than a thousand euros a piece, these were intended to guarantee my mother's lifelong financial security. As for me, well, seeing as life had endowed me with an exceptional husband, he declared that evening in his immense clairvoyance... I didn't need a thing!

Atropine.

I realised that for a year now I'd been having difficulty going up stairs without stopping to catch my breath... Not that it was an issue, I told myself, given that I spent all day in front of a computer.

It was only once I started lugging bags of hash from one place to another that my under-performing heart became a problem. My visit to the cardiologist only confirmed what I already knew.

If you can no longer find a way to work or to enjoy yourself, you may as well pack your bags and check out, my father had said to us that evening...

To see him swallowing his oysters with the appetite of an ogre, it was hard to believe he had already planned his death. Truth be told, though, it had been a good fifteen years already that he had been chewing over his plan. Since the business with Martine, actually – that was when life started to lose its interest for him.

Martine was the daughter of a soldier, blonde with green eyes, an apprentice hairdresser, who had the bad idea to die from an overdose at the age of seventeen in August 1969, in the toilets of a casino in Bandol. Her death was followed by a hysterical campaign orchestrated by the Gaullist politician, Alain Peyrefitte, who pointed the finger at hashish, LSD and heroin as the root of all evils: that is, pornography, homosexuality, miniskirts, the degeneracy of the younger generation and the decline in moral values generally... In short, the chaos of May 1968. This tightening of the screw towards the right led to a law criminalising the importation and sale of drugs that, until then, had not caused anybody any problems seeing it was the *French connection* that was supplying 90% of America's heroin. Mondiale was thus deprived of the most lucrative branch of its operations.

The second great blow to his morale came in 1974 with Djibouti's independence. That French enclave, where he would go whenever he had a moment and where he had set up an office, reminded him of his colonial Tunisia. During the years of French presence, Djibouti was (and, by the way, still is) a nest of crooks – laundering banks, soldiers' brothels, weapons-stuffed containers en route to the African interior, alcohol and cocaine destined for the Persian Gulf. The place was rife with Corsicans, Italian pieds-noirs and Lebanese, all of whom knew my father and in whose company he felt completely at home. He made a lot of money there, but Independence cost him a fortune. I remember seeing him one Sunday, angrily burning bags and bags of French Afar and Issa bank notes in the leaf pit on *The Estate*.

To lose his patch a second time was too much; after that he was never the same. The speed limits on the motorway cost him his Porsche, after he was done doing 260. He was forced to buy a pathetic, dirty grey, salesrep car which made him sad just to look at it, and which my mother would climb into with a disdainful pout… And then the Left came to power in 1981, and with them the solidarity tax on wealth, the 39-hour week, retirement at 60… All the so-called 'protective public policy provisions' aimed at defending society's most vulnerable members against large predators like him – the sort of man who might haul a driver out through twenty centimetres of open car window to head butt them for something as trivial as having cut in front of him.

Either you adapt, or you die… When it came to living in a country run by sermonising teachers, well, at some point he chose the latter.

After taking his leave from the two of us that day in 1986 at La Coupole, he left for Djibouti; and there, because he loved the Red Sea, wooden sailing boats and the books of his childhood friend, Henry de Monfreid, he cast off. Two months later, they found him dead, still sitting on the bridge of his boat, his body turned towards the sun.

He didn't commit suicide, he allowed himself to die to the beat of his own drum and at a time that suited him. We understood and we shed no tears.

There was a second bizarre thing that happened to me around that time, and I still can't get it out of my mind… A real-life plot twist of the sort I had been waiting for in vain for years.

It unfolded at *Les Eoliades*.

Ever since they had moved Monsieur Léger to our

floor, he would give a small yelp, calling out to his wife every time she went past his room. It was a super irritating little noise that reminded you of the sound baby llamas make calling after their mothers. A feeble, questioning *mmm-mmm*. Horrible!

She would stand there looking at her husband, stationed outside his door sometimes for ages, but all the poor man's frantic efforts to penetrate the thick fog of her memories were in vain, and at some point Madame would suddenly head off with her Zimmer frame on her path around the floor, forgetting why she had stopped. It was this that would make him weep, round after round, all day long. I'd already told the Léger children many times that it had been a bad idea to put their two parents on the same floor, but they found it more practical when they visited and apparently believed it was beneficial for their father to see his wife.

On 20 January, at around 8pm, when the carers were busy getting the whole floor to bed, I heard an unusual noise coming from Monsieur Léger's room, followed by the infamous *mmmmmmmm*, only this time it was continuous and he was singing.

I was very distracted – there had been no envelope that morning at the Romainville Monoprix under my Chamonix Oranges, and my hash hadn't moved from the storage locker at the pool – so I wasn't paying much attention. What's more, my mother was being particularly bloody trying that evening, asking me for a *frozen* Diet Coke, not a *cold* one, like the one she was refusing to drink and had deliberately poured onto the floor. After mopping it up, I went off to fetch another can from the dispenser, passing Monsieur Léger's room on the way, lost in thought and not looking in to see why he had been singing continuously for twenty minutes. When I came back with my can, a carer was calling for help. Monsieur Léger was just finishing off strangling his wife, using his one good arm, holding her in the crook between the upper- and the fore-arm. The carer was trying to make him loosen his grip, but he had his wife too firmly around the neck. By the time I got to the room, it was too late. Madame Léger was dead.

With my mother, I had truly thought I'd entered some sort of inner circle of Hell for the Elderly. Apparently not, I told myself, as I looked at the aged assassin singing away.

'*Ikh vil ein coca…*' came the shout from the neighbouring room. My mother. She was still with us.

The third event took place in my stairwell.

On the last Saturday of that unforgettable January, my neighbour from across the landing was marrying off her twenty-year old daughter with the extravagant display of wealth you would expect from a Chinese wedding. White limousine parked outside the building, an abundance of flowers worthy of a mafia godfather in the hall and stairwell … Families going up and down for hours to demonstrate their allegiance and hand their cash-filled envelopes to Madame Fò, whose door was open to receive them.

All of a sudden, I heard yelling. Through the peephole

at my front door, I saw a gang of four extremely fast and aggressive black guys descend on the guests, throwing punches and snatching bags, and showing no hesitation whatsoever at bashing up women and the elderly in order to get their hands on Madame Fò's cash. Three of them burst into my neighbour's place to steal all her money, while the fourth kept lookout, his back to my door. Acting on pure reflex, I grabbed my weapon, went out and aimed my revolver at the jaw of the guy closest to me, a kid barely fifteen years old who stared at me, panic-stricken. Everything froze. There was screaming in Chinese from all around. I don't understand that language, but I did know they all wanted me to pull the trigger.

'Hand over the bags and get out of here before they lock the doors on you for good.'

And they left, running.

I was shaking like a leaf, but not Madame Fò. She readjusted her outfit and thanked me, solemnly.

'Not first time. Nobody like Chinese. Police never help us. Thank you.'

We each went back to our own place.

To quote that rather impenetrable Chinese proverb: *talk doesn't cook rice.*

Poor Monsieur Léger was put under formal investigation for murder and placed under court supervision for having cut short, in his own way, the decline of his much-loved wife. (How has this country lost all sense of the absurd?)

Since he refused to eat, he ended up being thrown

out of *Les Eoliades* by the director, and wound up in the care of Nurse Ratched who intubated him to force-feed him, and eventually finished him off by puncturing his oesophagus.

Then, half way through February, a copy of the title deed to the apartment on Rue Monge dropped into my letter box. I had paid 60,000 euros for a piece of real estate worth 700,000.

When I opened the letter, I plonked myself down on the floor of my entrance hall, as breathless as if I had just run a long race. Through hard work and a few trips to Switzerland, I had managed to reconstitute my father's savings. I'd now converted more than two million euros into pink diamonds, and I was the owner of two apartments, one for each of my girls. I could stop now.

The Léger daughter with the eyes that sparkled at the thought of money, realising that the property had reverted and that she would not have a cent of inheritance, refused to leave me alone, to the point where I had to call her brother to get the harassment to stop.

'She's got to stop calling and telling me I'm a filthy thief!'

'I've told her to drop it, but she doesn't want to hear it.'

'Listen, I'm an honest person, and I'm sure, knowing the police as I do, that you must have made your own little enquiries about me… I don't have to take this, especially seeing as my own mother is still here. I'm relying on you to make it stop, because if it doesn't, I'm going to have to file a complaint.'

'Yes, yes, yes… I'll handle it,' he said, sighing.

'I'm not a monster and I'm prepared to make a gesture provided you take care of it. Open a savings account in your nephews' names and I'll give them each 20,000 euros to pay for their studies. There, I can't do more than that.'

'That's already huge. You're a good woman!'

Yes, yes, I know, I'm a good woman.

So… Scotch, Momo, Lizard, Chocapic and the others – my gang – they had all been arrested. I found out from Philippe who'd invited me to spend a weekend with his son at Le Touquet. That suited me. Everything suited me. I was on cloud nine.

Philippe and I were not sharing a room, we just ate and swam in the hotel pool together. I'm not going to lie, I was very happy for those two days, walking along the beach with DNA and pretending I had a family.

My mother, who had occupied the planet for ninety-two years, finally died on 28 March 2017.

Thinking she was doing the right thing, Anta had combed her mop of grey hair so it looked like a halo around her head. It was ridiculous. My girls and I were sitting around her bed looking at her, and all of a sudden, all three of us burst out laughing.

Despite everything, I knew they were sad because they really did love their grandmother. I can't deny that she had always been there to look after them when I'd had to work forty-eight hours straight without setting foot in the house. Part of the money my father had left her, she had blown on them in a whirlwind of flouncy dresses and holidays on the other side of the world, buying them all the clothes I refused to pay for. Everything nice they did during their childhood, they did with her, while I was busy struggling to keep my head above water. Assuming she was capable of feeling anything, I think she loved them a hundred times more than she loved me, her only daughter, whom she saw as the enemy of her happiness and who represented everything that was hard in life. To hell with Patience and all her misfortunes, the spectacle of her misery offends me! *This is all such a bore... let's go to the sales!* She was a selfish mother, and horribly unjust.

Since we didn't have a family plot, she had asked to be cremated, with her ashes scattered in a department store.

The girls and I carried out her final wishes, selecting the Galeries Lafayette. After the ceremony at the crematorium, we divided the contents of the urn between us. I chose to scatter my share through the boutiques of her favourite designers. If you happened to find a bit of grey dust or some strange little bits of matter at the bottom of your Dior, Nina Ricci or Balenciaga suit pockets from the Spring-Summer 2017 collection – that was my mother. As for my daughters, I saw them gently sprinkle the rest over the perfume department as they stood side by side at the balustrade under the stained glass dome.

To finish up, we went off to stuff ourselves at Angelina's tearoom in the bra section.

It's hard to imagine a more *girly* celebration. For once my mother would have been satisfied.

*

I took advantage of her death to launder some of my money through her estate, and also accepted Colette Fò's offer to buy my apartment. Despite my act of valour, she didn't offer me a discount, but she did say this, which floored me:

'You can leave drug in basement until you find other place.'

I stood there, speechless.

'I thought you didn't even see me,' I stammered.

She smiled. 'In the building we call you *the phantom*. But you less phantom now. Lot less.'

She invited me in for some tea and told me a little about her life. She was seven years younger than me and, like many of the Chinese in Belleville, came from Wenzhou province, a small port of eight million inhabitants, four hundred kilometres from Shanghai. She was definitely not a widow as I had imagined, and somewhere in China, there existed a Mr Fò whom she never saw and who produced counterfeit spare auto parts that she flogged to mechanics, thereby explaining the red-white-and-blue plastic Tati bags weighing two tonnes that she too was always lugging around in the lift. Her family also owned a hair factory which made extensions that were imported to France and resold to Africans in Paris who then sold them on to their country of origin. Every cent earned in China, Africa or France was reinvested in Pari Mutuel Urbain betting licences for bar-tabacs, giant money laundering machines, and from there into real estate.

You may call us wops, vulgar foreigners, outsiders – but tremble, good people, for we shall crush you all!

She had arrived twelve years ago, reuniting with a distant uncle who was already living in our building. She had two children: a girl born in China who was now about twenty and whom she had not seen grow up, and another born in France who was twelve and with whom she had been pregnant as an immigrant. As soon as she became a French citizen, she had brought over the whole family, one at a time, including cousins and elderly family members. She had chosen her first name because Colette was the only French woman writer she had studied in Wenzhou, when she had learned our language for a year.

She was a very pleasant woman, and I was annoyed with myself for not having tried to get to know her before moving out.

I trusted her completely with my life story, as her own experiences mirrored those of my family. She asked a few questions about my job as a translator and we discovered that we had something unexpected in common, namely we both earned a living by dealing exclusively with Arabs. Her long-term dream was to break into the Maghreb market with her spare auto parts. Given that I spoke the language and had already proven myself as a business woman, she predicted a glowing relationship ahead. In a gesture of friendship, I gave her my father's weapon, after making her promise not to use it herself but to give it to a bodyguard to protect her friends and family at their next celebration.

Finally, we went down to the basement to move what remained of my stock into an old boiler room; that's to say, exactly 463 kilos of hash, taking into account the samples I had distributed.

'What you do with that?'

'I don't know. You don't know anybody who might be interested? I don't need it anymore; I have enough money for my small family.'

'Drugs, in China, death penalty. Just bring problem.'

'I'll get rid of it, then.'

With the money from the sale of my apartment to the Fò family, I bought a second one on Rue Monge in the same building as the Léger's, which I moved into. So one morning in June, I left Belleville.

Philippe helped me pack my boxes and carry them down to the removal van.

When almost everything had been loaded up, and we were utterly dead on our feet, I made him a coffee. We sat on the remaining two boxes with DNA at our feet and I told him, with a hint of nostalgia, about the twenty-six years which had unfolded within those four walls. Suddenly he stood up to have a look through my cupboards.

'If you're looking for spoons, I've packed everything, they're all gone.'

'I'm hungry. I just feel like a little something to snack on.'

And he opened a cupboard where I had forgotten about fifteen or so packets of Chamonix Oranges.

I paled.

He opened one up happily and held it out to me.

'I guess you must really like these!'

'I was supposed to make an orange-flavoured tiramisu one day for one of my daughter's parties and I never got round to it, so I was stuck with all of those. I've been working my way through them one packet at a time before they go out of date.'

He drank his coffee in silence, and I saw his face change.

I carried on as if nothing had happened.

'I've always wondered who eats Chamonix Oranges. They're pretty disgusting as cakes go,' he said, quietly.

As in a near-death experience, all the clues I might have left in my wake flashed before me. I had caught sight of myself walking past windows a thousand times and I knew I was unrecognisable from the CCTV images when dressed as the Godmother. My business partners would never be able to identify me, except perhaps from my voice, but the authoritative tone I used when speaking Arabic would render even this difficult. And anyway, it was hardly France's finest intellects we were talking about! I had only ever taken taxis, and never from outside my place. And as for my exchanges in the supermarkets, there was nothing to identify me, apart from this business with the cakes. There was only one day, the day of the fiasco in the wedding dress department at Tati, which could put me in the frame, because somewhere on a street CCTV camera from four months ago, there would be me and DNA on his leash. There was also one false translation of an intercept, but I had handled it in such a way that you could think it was a misunderstanding and not a deliberate falsification. When I heard that Scotch and his gang had been arrested, I'd thrown out all my disguises and my money counter. I'd only ever handled the hash with gloves on – hash that couldn't be found, stashed away in a Chinese hidey-hole in the basement of the building. My money-laundering had been impeccable and the primary beneficiary of my largesse – a certain Detective Léger – would certainly not say anything to the contrary. As regards my comings and goings to Switzerland, I had always bought my ticket in cash at the counter at Gare de Lyon, using a fake name. And good luck to anyone trying to find my pink diamonds; they had all been inserted into lipsticks and hidden in my make-up bag. No, there was nothing except for those hideously sweet cakes with which Philippe was busy stuffing himself.

'What's the matter? Have they gone stale?'

He stared at me as if he thought he might be able to see right through to my brain.

'What?' I said, laughing.

DNA chose just that moment to come and rest his head on his thigh and beg for a pat; and right there, in the blink of an eye, he pretty much understood how I had managed to find the product to sell, accepted that he would never be able to prove it, and decided he wouldn't take any action.

I'm so sorry, my poor Philippe, for this little death I've inflicted upon you... but if only you'd been just a bit less honest...

'I'm going home, I don't feel too good,' he said.

And the man I saw leaving the apartment of my former life was a man who, in a fraction of a second, had aged a thousand years.

He never called me again. Nor I him.

The end of my adventure was not particularly interesting, even if it did result in an affair of State.

In order to dispose of the 463 kilos of hash I still had, I contacted the Tunisians being surveilled by the Central Bureau for Illicit Drug Traffic Control, explaining that I'd been given their number by the friend of a friend of my supposed son, who was hiding some hash in his bedroom which I absolutely had to get rid of. I loaded all my product into a van I'd rented through the commercial vehicle-sharing service, Utilib, using the card of a dead Chinese man…

This time it was a whining, old, badly-dressed Godmother who ventured forth onto the streets. 'My son… you know, his papa was killed by the Armed Islamic Group of Algeria… I'm raising him all on my own and he won't listen to me… not to anything I say!'

I was so persuasive those guys were seriously worried for me.

'I don't care if he kills me, but as long as I'm alive, he is not going to prison for doing drugs. Before all this, he used to be a good student, he was kind… So, take it, take the lot, I don't want to see it in our home anymore!'

They didn't waste any time hanging around, and left with my hash, their car loaded up to the point that the under-carriage was almost dragging along the ground. With a huge sense of relief, I watched them disappear.

A week later, I was summoned by the examining magistrate, who wanted to speak to the Benabdelaziz's driver. He was in the corridor, seated and handcuffed, waiting for me, his accredited translator.

'I know it was you who took our product...'

'Me? But what would I do with it? I have done my own research, though. I've listened to a lot of dealers. It took some time, but I know now who picked it up... And I think they should pay for what they've done because I was very fond of Khadija. It's the Tunisians. I've got their name, their address, their phone number... I can give you everything.'

Et voilà.

There was some fall-out with the dealers-informants-police. Some deaths. Some cops in the slammer. A big fat scandal. I'd had a good nose: those guys were indeed hybrid dealers bred by the Central Bureau for Drug Control.

The rest of the story is all there in the papers; there's no need for me to go over it again.

No clean policing without dirty policing, they say. Well then, let's give these state-sanctioned dealer-bureaucrats a taste of their own laws.

Mambo

So what now?

I'm feeling quite light-headed at the thought of all these lives opening up before me. The future is wide open. I could go back to France to work with Madame Fò, wait for grandchildren to arrive and take them to the park where I'll watch them climb on the monkey bars... Or, like an uprooted plant, tossed about by the wind, make my way from one fireworks display to another until I'm all shrivelled up and for whatever reason am no longer able to continue. Or I could do as my mother did, and pretend to be busy, buy lots of useless stuff, play with it, grow bored with it, throw it away, return it, resell it – always in a hurry because the shops are about to close... Or else take my father's approach, stop looking after myself and die, drowning in the rose pink sky at the end of a day like this one... Or I could simply live for myself and for the joy of seeing myself alive.

We'll see: let's just say that for the time being, I'm lying fallow. I've come back to the only place in the world where people were expecting me, to Muscat in the Sultanate of Oman. I've settled into the hotel where my life jumped off the rails like the diamond in a record player jumps from one groove to another, from a mellow song to a ghastly jingle. Unlike the little fireworks collector's palace, the Belvedere, this place hasn't changed a bit.

These days, what I love to do more than anything is slide my chair as close as possible to the window looking out over the bay. I can stay there for hours, contemplating the perfect tableau of colours composed by the pink carpet of my room, the blond wood of the window framing the bay, and the sun like an orange ball drowning in the blue light… and with that I'm replete.

It's time to leave now, before it gets too dark. I've had to wait for nightfall because it's quite a drive out to Petroleum Cemetery and DNA doesn't cope well with the heat now that he's getting on.

The way things turned out, my husband and I knew each other for such a short time, and it was so long ago. But I think he would have liked the woman I've become. I've arranged a fireworks display for this evening out at the cemetery, just for the two of us. I didn't stint. I've chosen sparkly starbursts and bombettes that will light up the desert sky with enormous, orange-centred pink chrysanthemums.

And here's a little story to finish.

It happened one evening when we were travelling together in Valparaìso. We wandered into a deserted cabaret bar called the Cinzanno Club. The decoration was dated and kitsch, and the elderly members of a tropical music orchestra were fast asleep on the stage, slumped on chairs facing out to small, empty, candle-lit tables. All of a sudden, the leader of the ensemble, an old guy with dyed hair and a body bowed by arthritis, noticed us at the door. He snapped himself upright and shouted '*mambo*', vigorously shaking his pineapple-shaped maracas to wake up his musicians and breathe some sort of desperate energy into them.

'*Mambo.*'

Acknowledgements

Thank you to those translators and interpreters of the Palais de Justice in Paris who assisted me, and whose names I have deliberately not disclosed so that they may continue to do their work.

Hannelore Cayre is an award-winning French novelist, screenwriter and director, as well as a practising criminal lawyer. Her most recent novel, *The Godmother* (*La Daronne*) has been made into a feature film starring Isabelle Huppert, and is scheduled for release in early 2020. She lives in Paris.